THE WALL OF SHAME-EXCLUSIVE COVERAGE

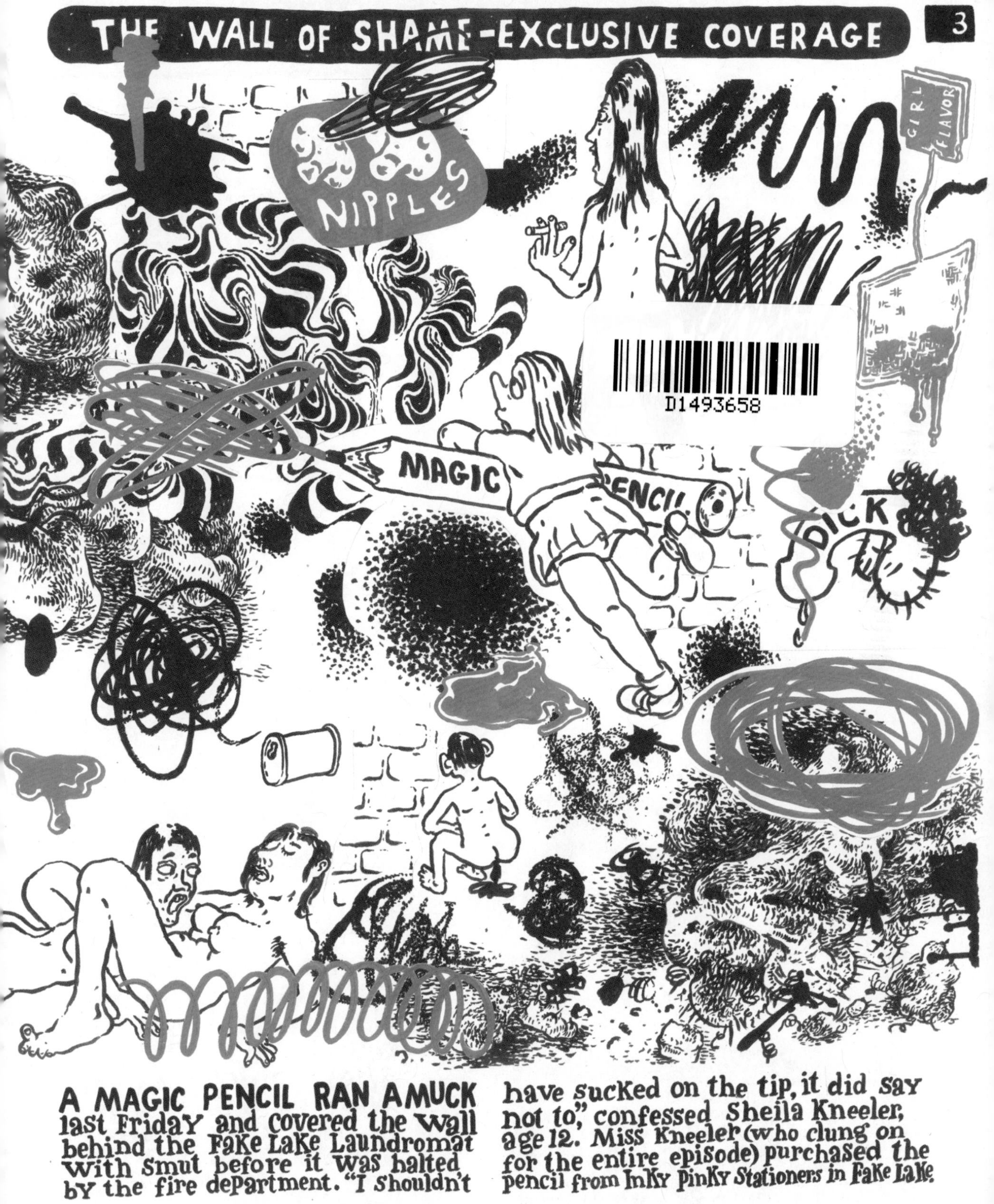
NIPPLES
GIRL FLAVOR
MAGIC
PENCIL
DICK

A MAGIC PENCIL RAN AMUCK last Friday and covered the wall behind the Fake Lake Laundromat with smut before it was halted by the fire department. "I shouldn't have sucked on the tip, it did say not to," confessed Sheila Kneeler, age 12. Miss Kneeler (who clung on for the entire episode) purchased the pencil from Inky Pinky Stationers in Fake Lake.

YOUR LOCAL NEWS

NOBODY'S BUDGING

The impasse between Mr. Unwavering and Mr. Clampdown continues in the center of Main Street Fake Lake. Neither party has given more than a few inches in the five months since the men collided.

IT STINKS

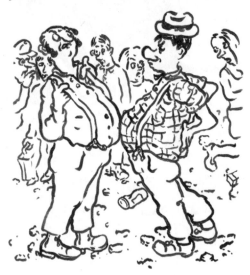

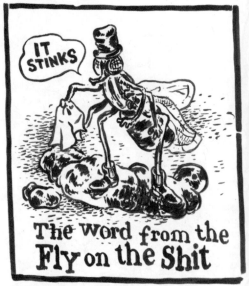

The word from the Fly on the Shit

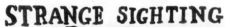

STRANGE SIGHTING

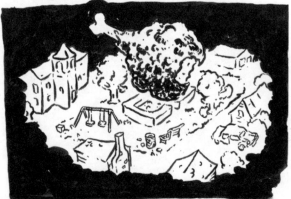

A giant chicken drumstick was observed hovering above the green yesterday. It was positively identified from a bit of fallen batter, as originating in the Greasy Spoon Diner. Authorities would like to know how the cook staff got it into orbit and on a private note, the editor would like to know if it could come with gravy?

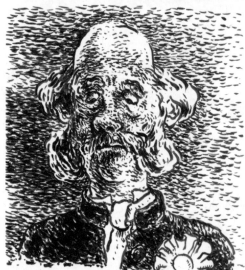

THE MAYORWITHAL

Mayor Dundoing did nothing today with consummate flourish and was applauded roundly by City Council after which everyone went for a slap-up lunch at the Curmudgeon's Club and got sodden with drink and had to sleep it off in chambers.

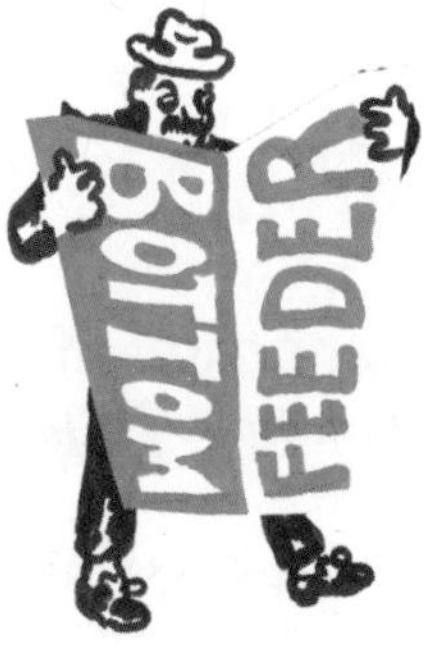
BOTTOM
FEEDER

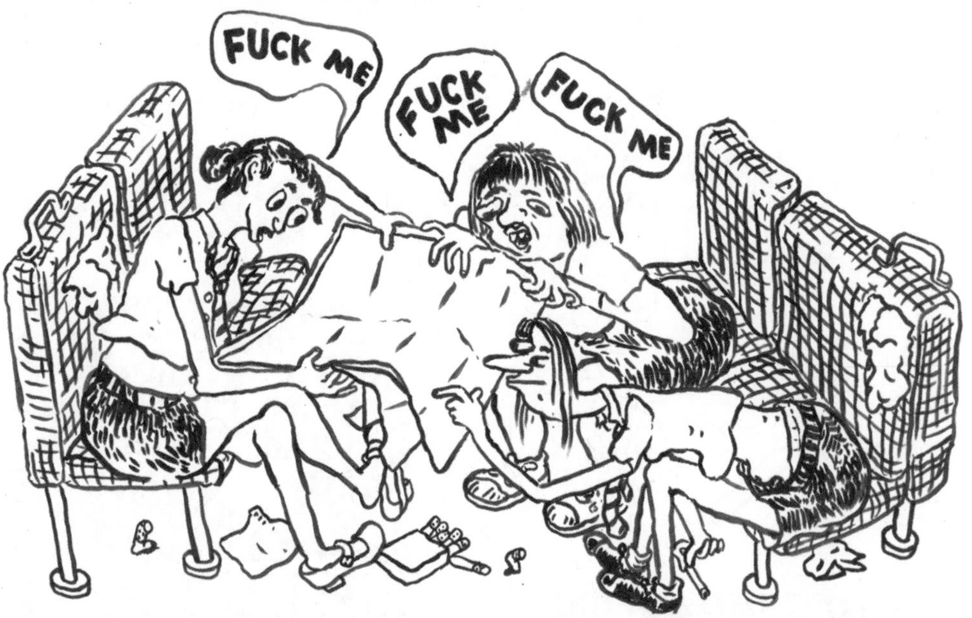
FUCK ME
FUCK ME
FUCK ME

SCHOOLGIRLS FROM ST. ALLSKIRTS PERUSE THE FAKE LAKE BOTTOM FEEDER ON THE TRAIN HOME

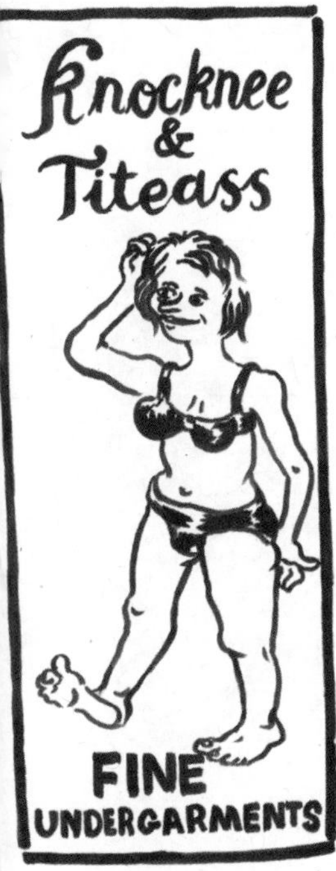
Knocknee
&
Titeass
FINE
UNDERGARMENTS

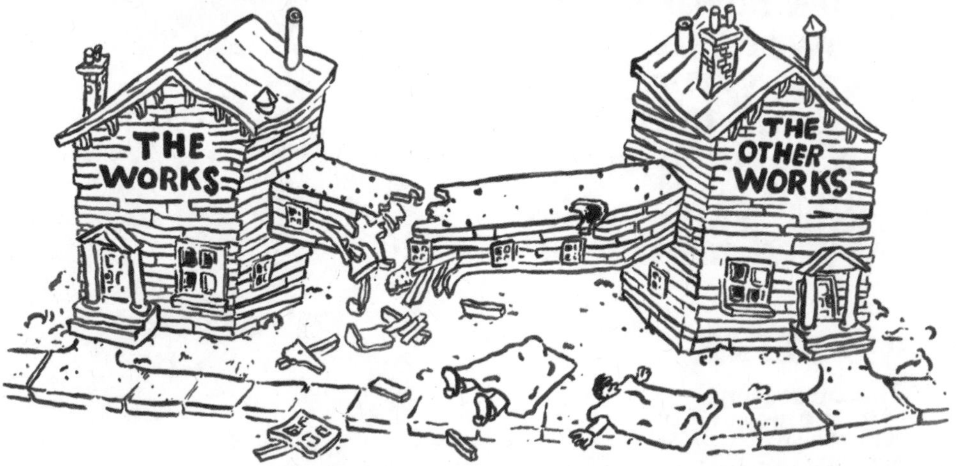
THE
WORKS
THE
OTHER
WORKS

Connecting Walk Collapses

It came as no surprise that the connecting walk between The Works and The Other Works collapsed Monday night. The connection has long been suspected of harboring pernicious dry rot and people are forever stomping up and down when they get to the middle just to see it bounce. Fatally injured in the accident were Mr. Jumpforjoy and Mr. Giddywithmirth, both junior employees of The Works. They will hardly be missed.

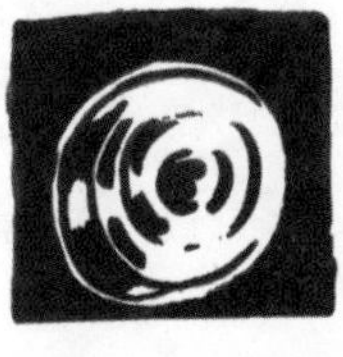

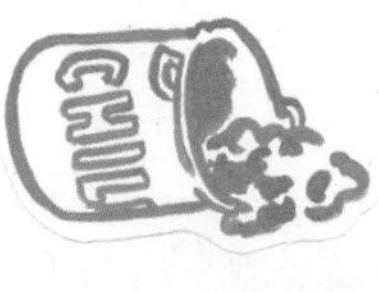
CHILI

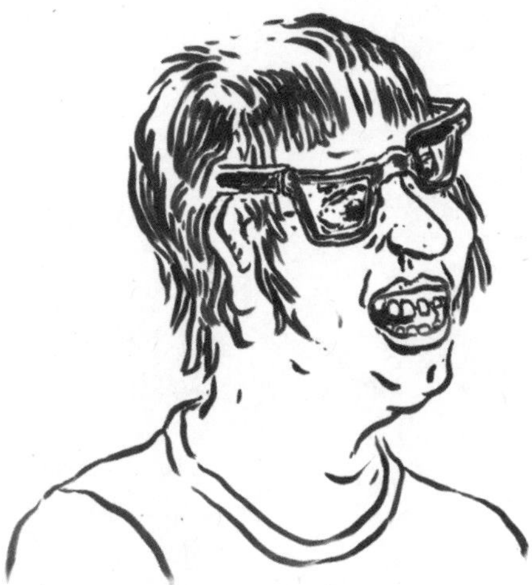

Tire StacK Still Smouldering

It has been thirty Years now since the tire Pile at the edge of town caught fire and it still continues to belch smoKe. Authorities are wondering if it is not just possible that some some persons are secretly re-lighting it.

Editor's note: I am still belching smoKe after eating the chili at the Greasy Spoon Diner last month. Perhaps they are dumping the leftovers there.

NEW LIBRARIAN APPOINTED

Mrs. Halfmarble vows to cracK down on late borrowers and other library wrongdoers. "I'm going to come down hard on 'em. I'm going to break their fucKing balls. They're going to get marbleized!"

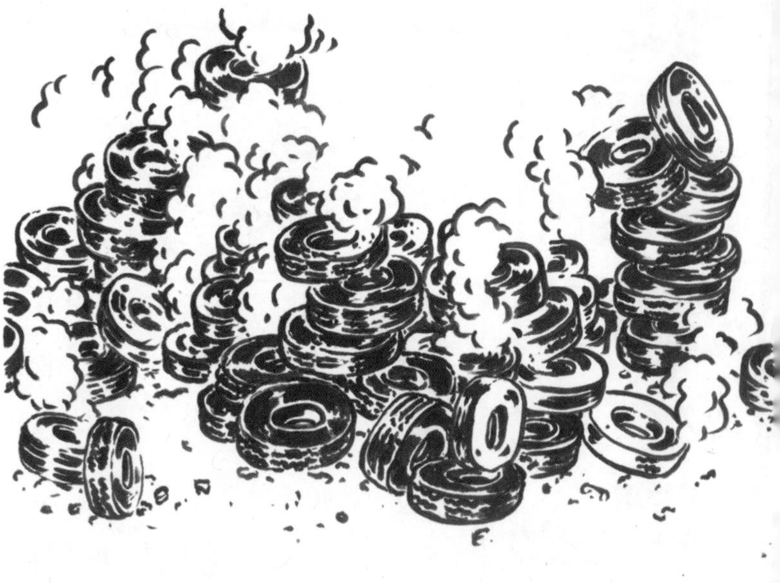

BIG STINK

The obnoxious smell emanating from the FaKe LaKe men's public toilets was deemed by authorities, after thorough investigation to be pee and we'll just have to put up with it.

Editor's note: Precision aim Gentlemen! That and a sprinKling of mothballs every so often. Or use the Ladies.

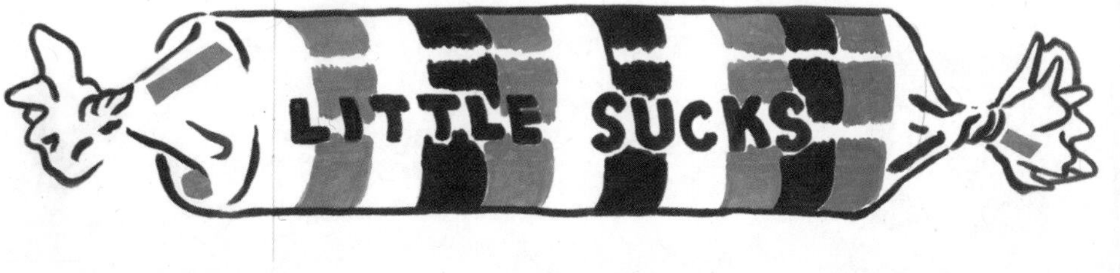
LITTLE SUCKS

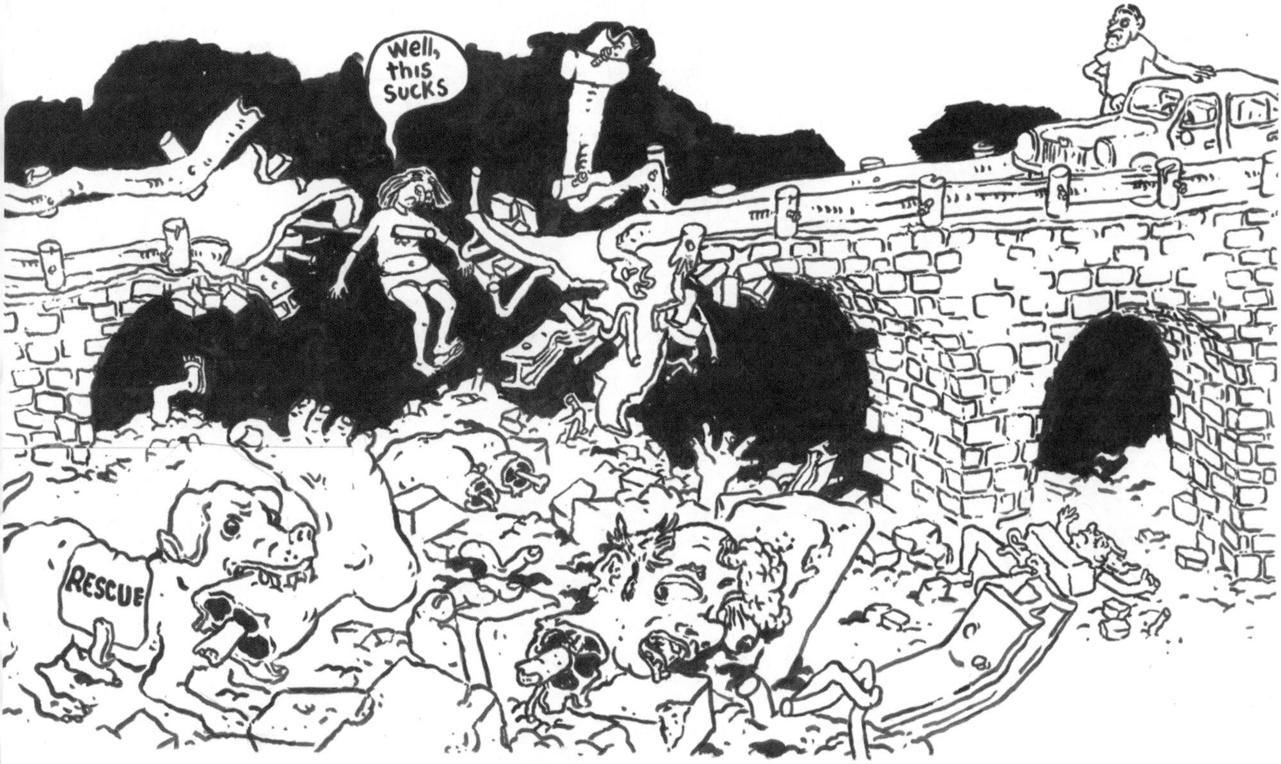
Well, this sucks
RESCUE

A STRONG FOOTING was obviously not what the Fake Lake Memorial Town Bridge was built on as users discovered on Sataurday when four of the five spans collapsed utterly leaving a mound of bloody rubble. Sniffer dogs sent to uncover the some fifteen buried people proved unreliable and could be observed gnawing on the sticky-outy bits of the victims.

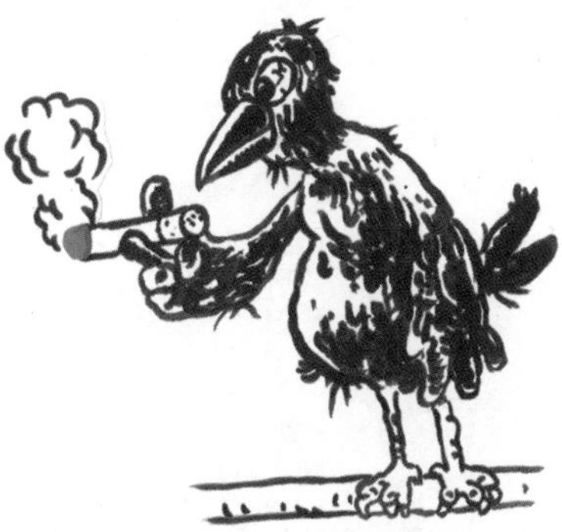

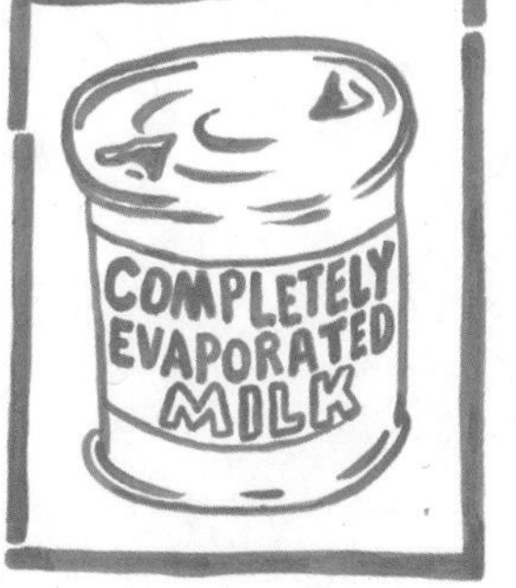
COMPLETELY EVAPORATED MILK

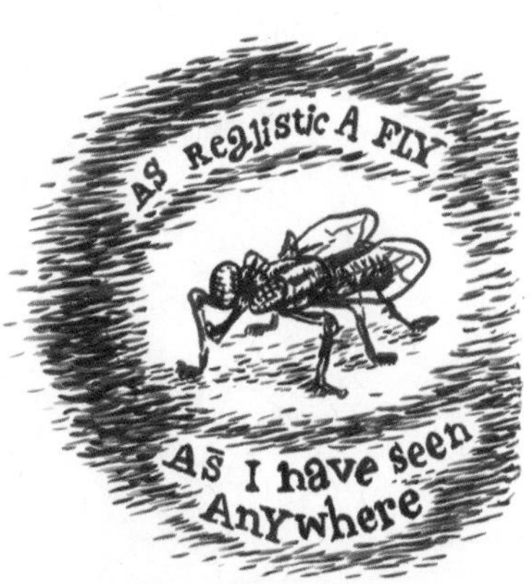
As Realistic A FLY
As I have seen AnYwhere

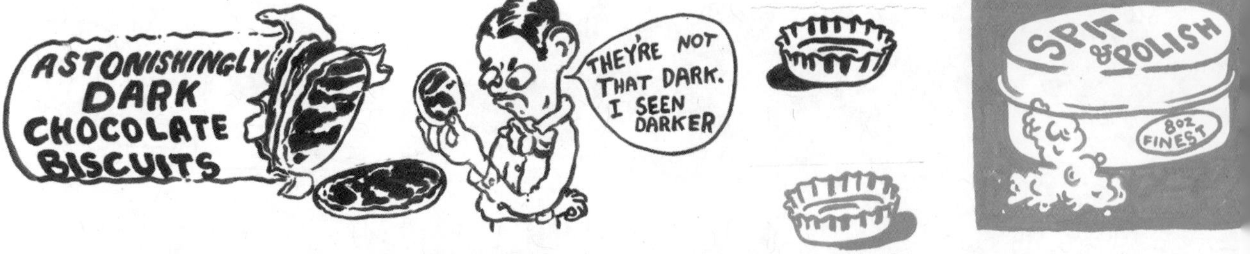
ASTONISHINGLY DARK CHOCOLATE BISCUITS
THEY'RE NOT THAT DARK. I SEEN DARKER
SPIT & POLISH
8oz FINEST

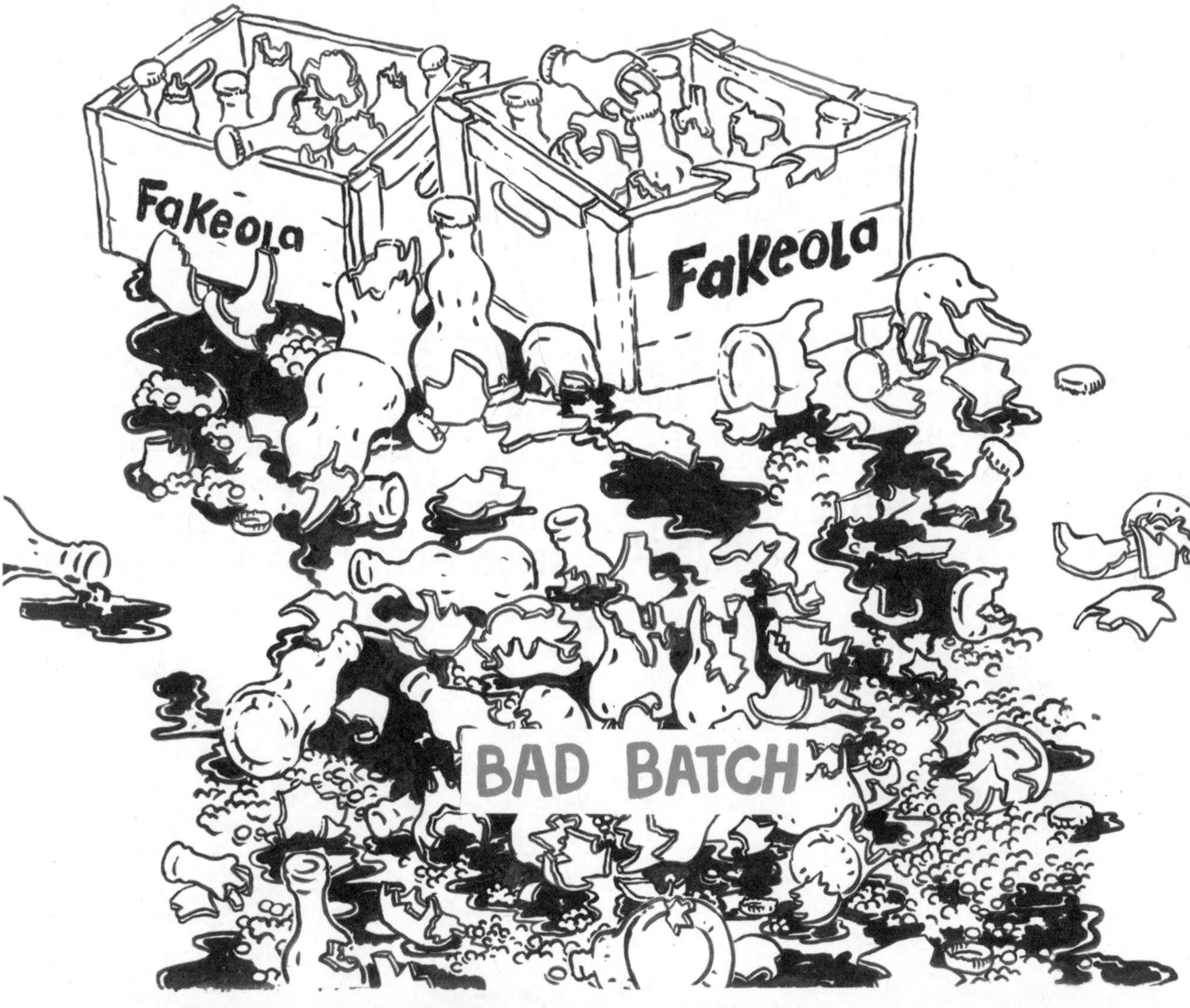
FaKeoLa
FaKeoLa
BAD BATCH

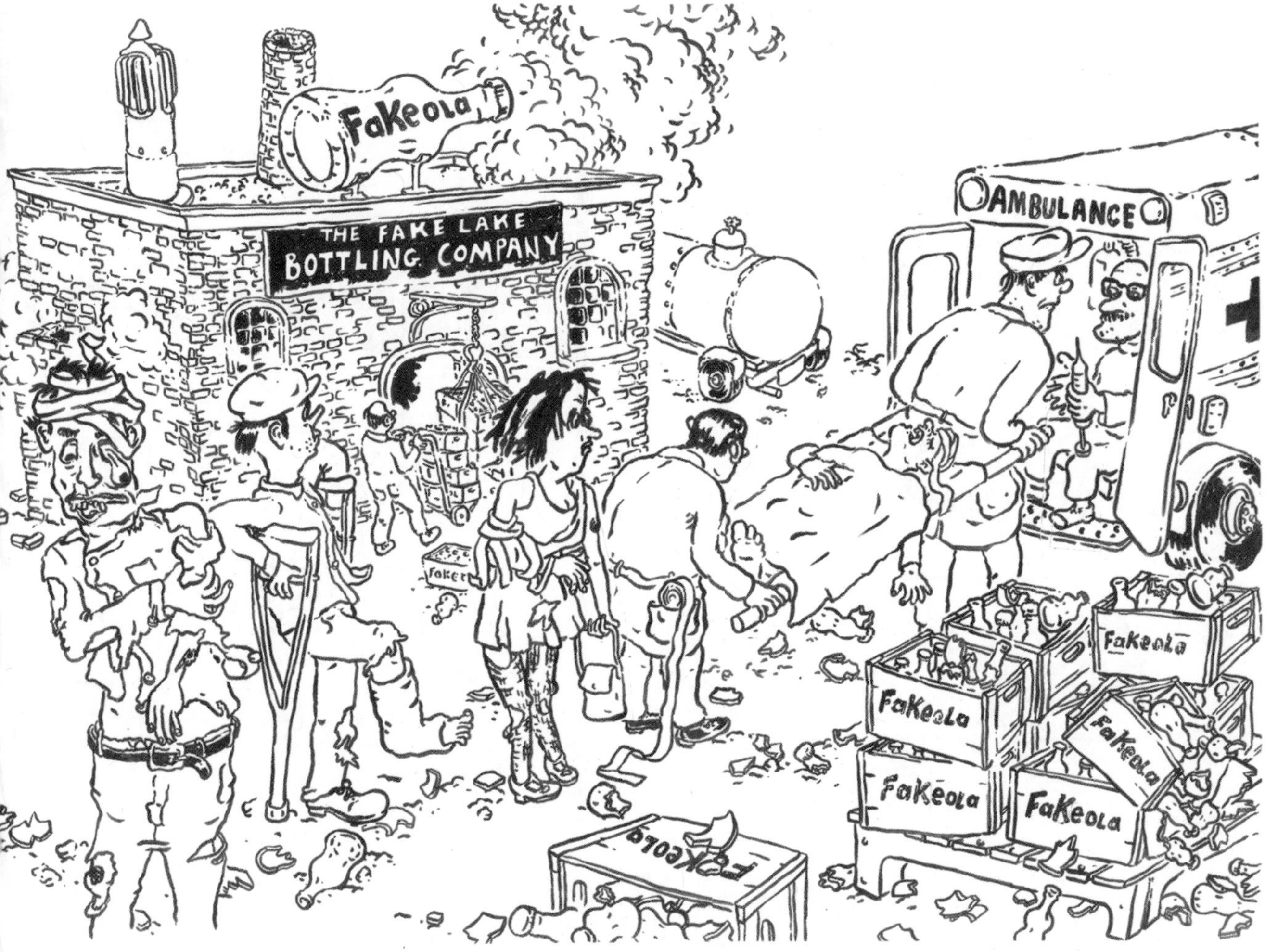
FaKeoLa
THE FAKE LAKE BOTTLING COMPANY
AMBULANCE
FaKeoLa
FaKeoLa
FaKeoLa
FaKeoLa
FaKeoLa
FaKeoLa

CARBONATION MISCALCULATION

1500 bottles of FaKeola exploded in the bottling plant Wednesday resulting in grievous injury to workers and a bloody great hole in the plant. Officials blamed the accident on an excess of gas. Workers said that the batch had just "gone off" and that it "stunk to high heaven" and that "we told them it was gonna blow".

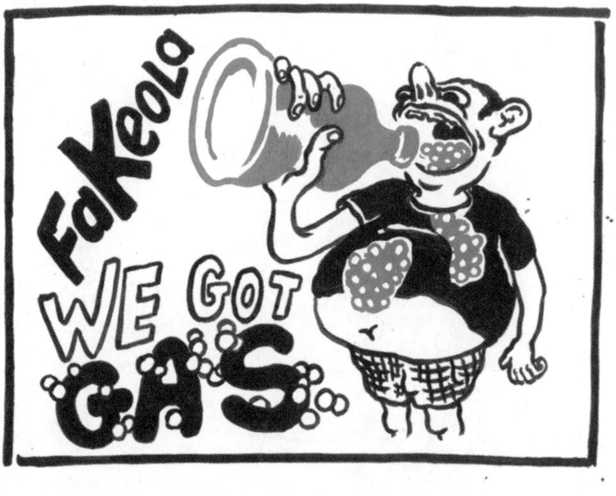
FaKeoLa
WE GOT
GAS

A TRAGIC MISSTEP

was what Albert Slump, 36, of Fake Lake, took on Tuesday, resulting in his being mostly melted away. Mr. Slump slipped while attempting to retrieve something or other from a vat of carbolic acid at the Fake Lake manufacturing plant.

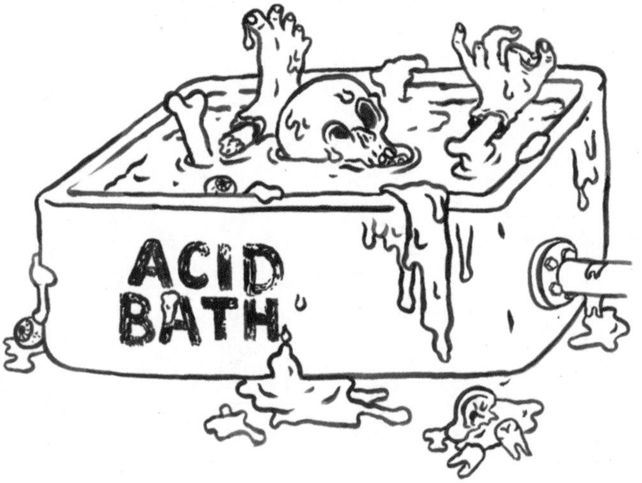
ACID
BATH

The Asshole of a Pencil

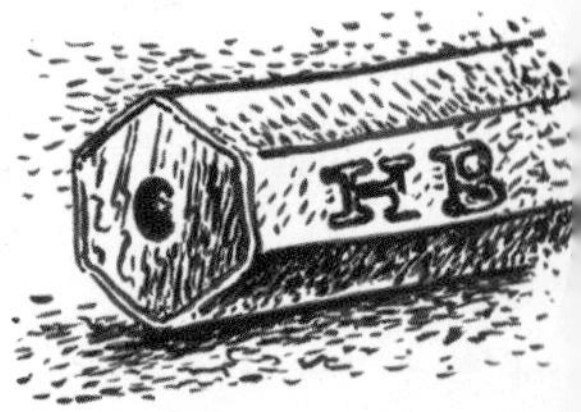
HB

SOPS-A-LOT

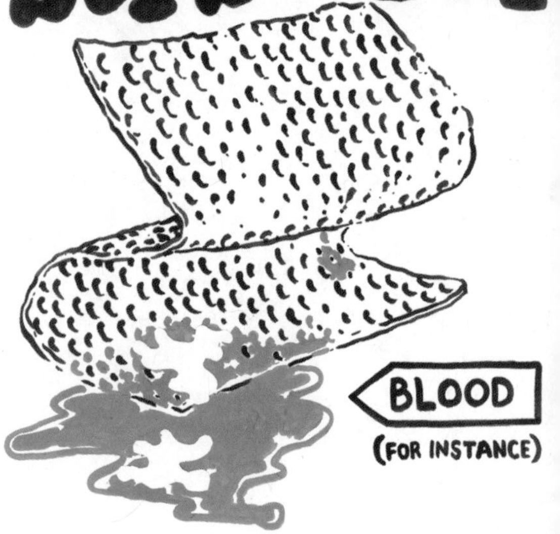
BLOOD
(FOR INSTANCE)

NO ONE FUCKS WITH OUR FLEET OF INDEPENDENT TRUCKS

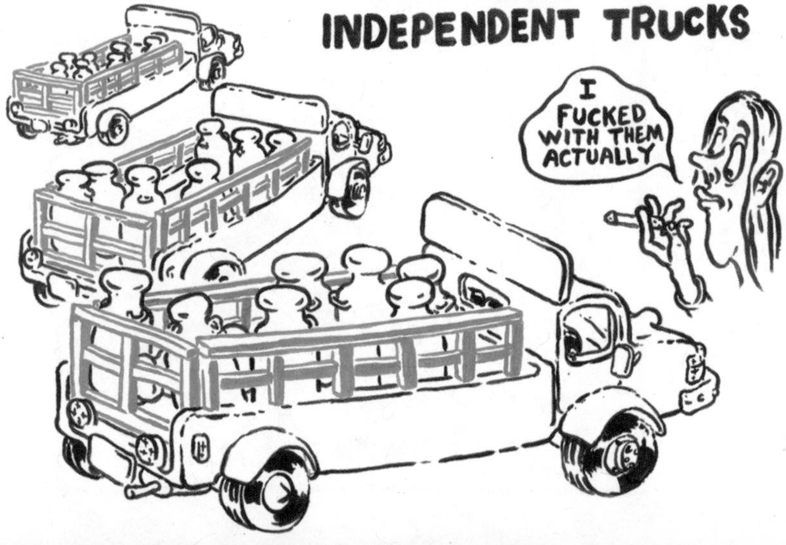
I FUCKED WITH THEM ACTUALLY

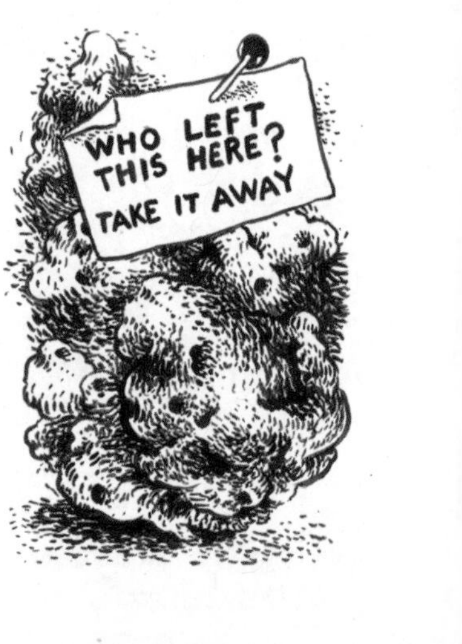
WHO LEFT THIS HERE?
TAKE IT AWAY

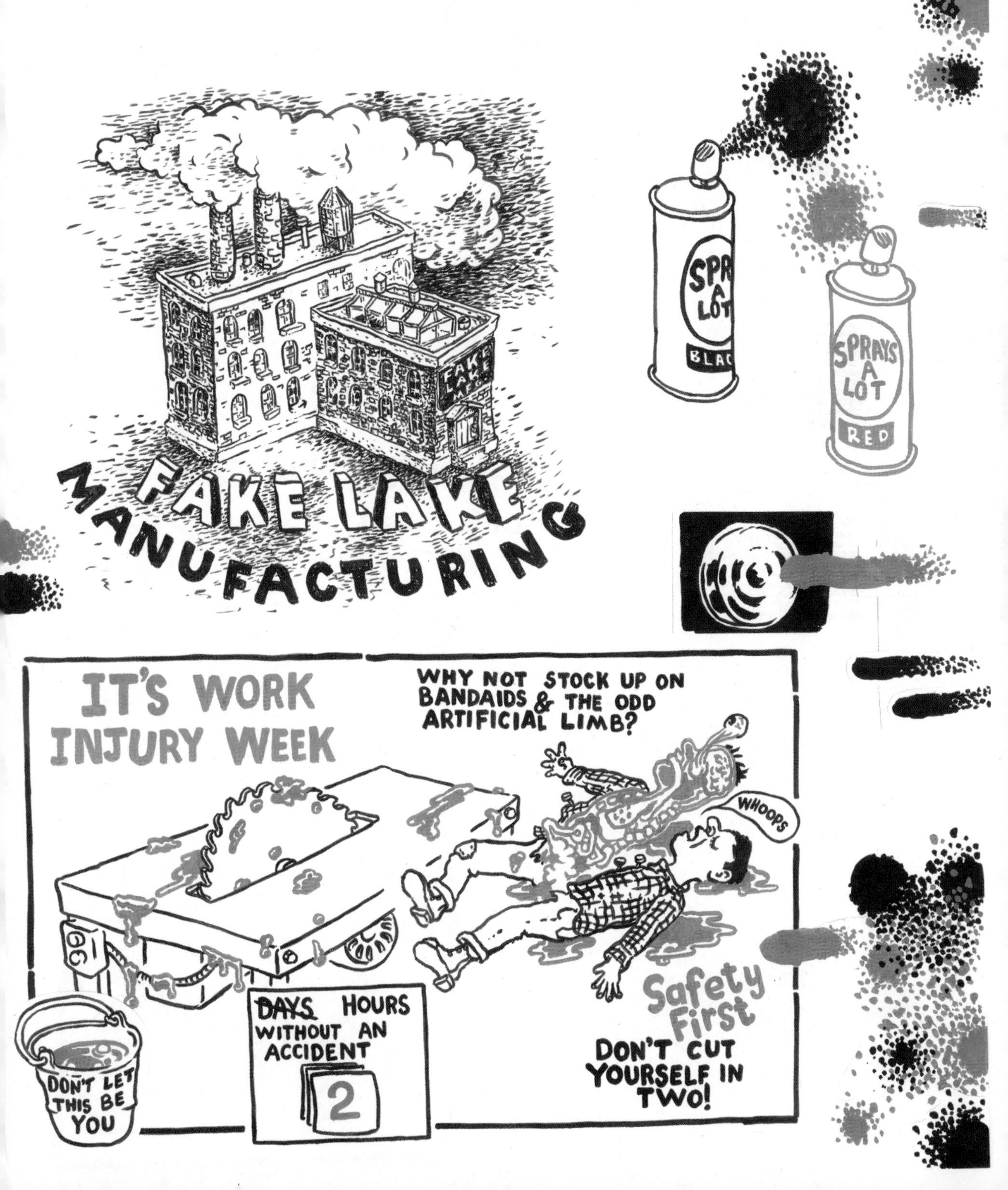
FAKE LAKE MANUFACTURING
SPR A LOT BLAC
SPRAYS A LOT RED
IT'S WORK INJURY WEEK
WHY NOT STOCK UP ON BANDAIDS & THE ODD ARTIFICIAL LIMB?
WHOOPS
Safety First
DON'T CUT YOURSELF IN TWO!
~~DAYS~~ HOURS WITHOUT AN ACCIDENT
2
DON'T LET THIS BE YOU

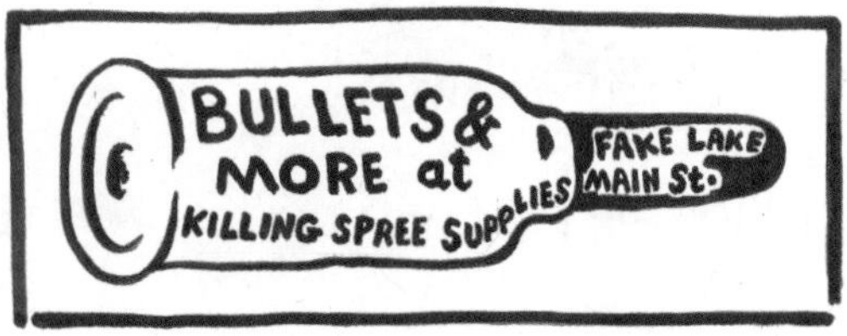
BULLETS & MORE at
KILLING SPREE SUPPLIES
FAKE LAKE MAIN St.

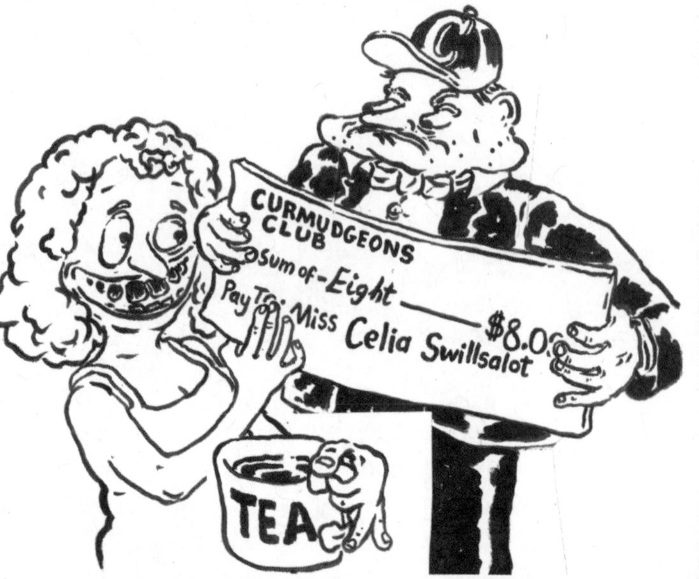
CURMUDGEONS CLUB
Sum of - Eight
Pay To: Miss Celia Swillsalot
$8.00
TEA

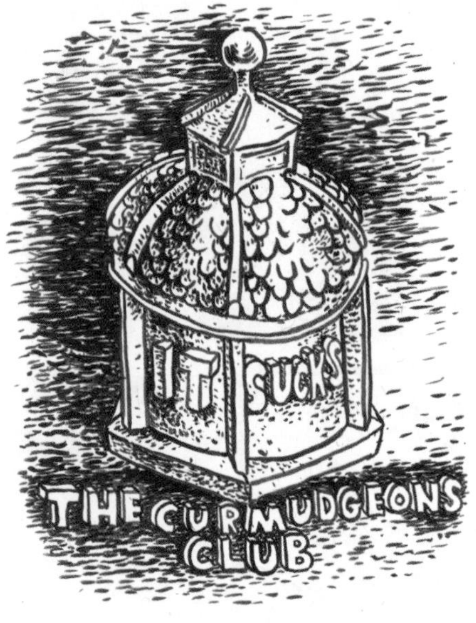
IT SUCKS
THE CURMUDGEONS CLUB

TANNIN RELIEF-WHEN BRUSHING FAILS

The Curmudgeon Club's annual Fuck-me-a-thon was held this Weekend raising a staggering sixteen dollars for people suffering from tea Stained teeth. takes no pleasure wha tsoevever in presenting a cheque for eight dollars to a delighted Miss Celia Swillsalot. (Editor's note: Try a swig of bleach Celia or just Keep your mouth closed.)

Above: Mr. Distemper

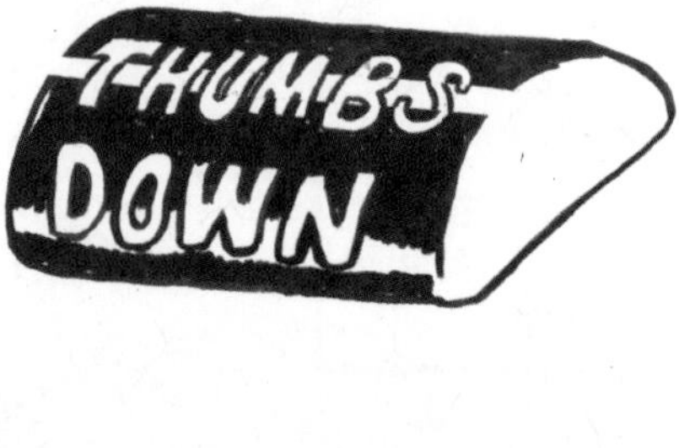
THUMBS DOWN

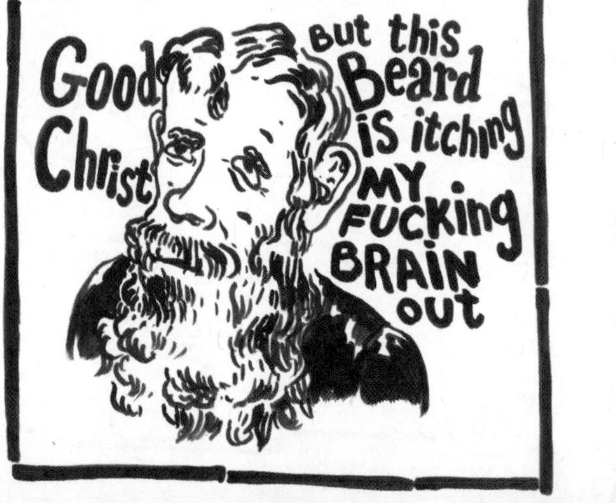
Good Christ
but this Beard is itching MY FUCKING BRAIN out

Conversation, as always is brisk at The Curmudgeon's Club. Here's a sample:

CURMUDGEON 1. - Fuck You!

CURMUDGEON 2. - Fuck You!
(LONG PAUSE)

CURMUDGEON 3. - Fuck You Butler!

BUTLER - Fuck You very much Sir!
(LONGER PAUSE)

CURMUDGEON 4. - Fuck You and fuck the China Dogs too!

China Dog 1. - Well fuck You!

China Dog 2. - Yeah, fuck you too!
(INORDINATELY LONG PAUSE)

CURMUDGEON 1. - Well fuck You!

CURMUDGEON 2. - Fuck You, you fucker You!

Etc..Etc.....

OUTDOOR ADVICE

#18: what to do if You get Your foot stuck in a bear trap. Yes, You will have to gnaw it off I'm afraid. Don't forget to reset the trap when You're done.

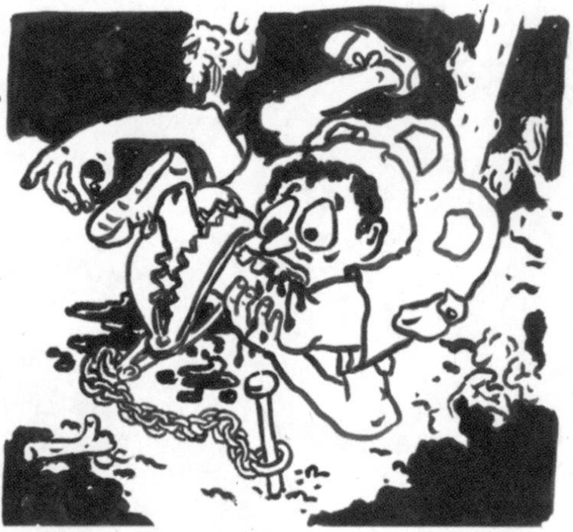

CONTAINS:
SWABS, SCABS, DRIBS, DRABS, SALMONELLA, BANK TELLER,

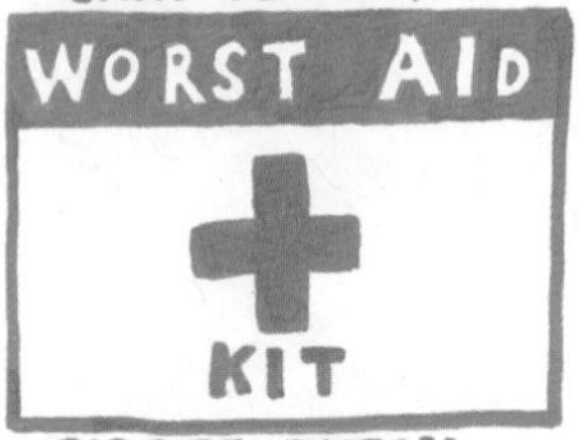
WORST AID
KIT

PIRATE PATCH, FUNNY HAT, LINT REMOVER.

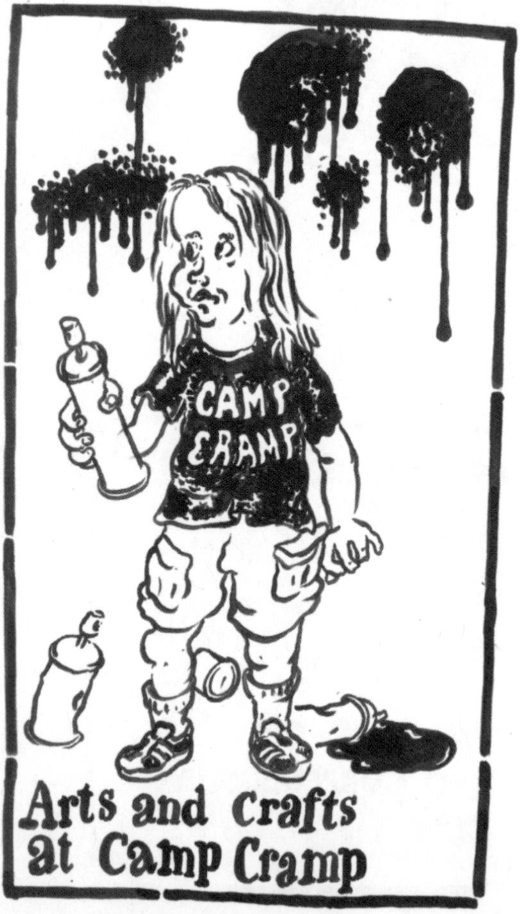
CAMP CRAMP

Arts and Crafts at Camp Cramp

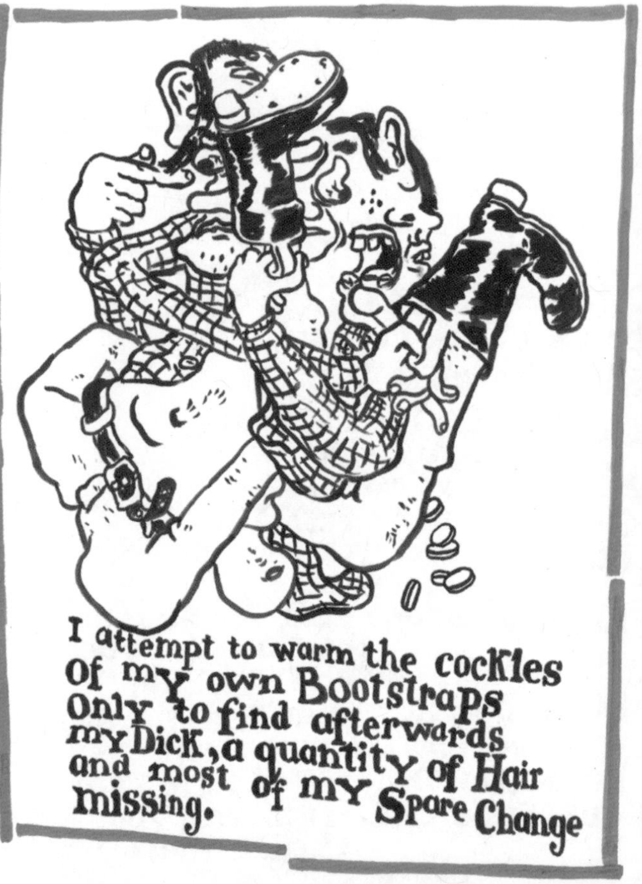

I attempt to warm the cockles of my own Bootstraps only to find afterwards my Dick, a quantity of Hair and most of my Spare Change missing.

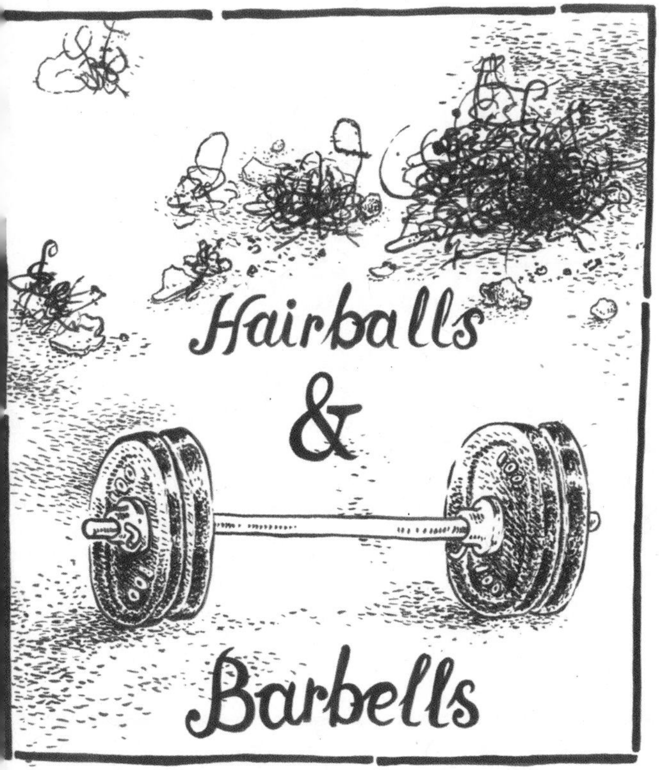
Hairballs
&
Barbells

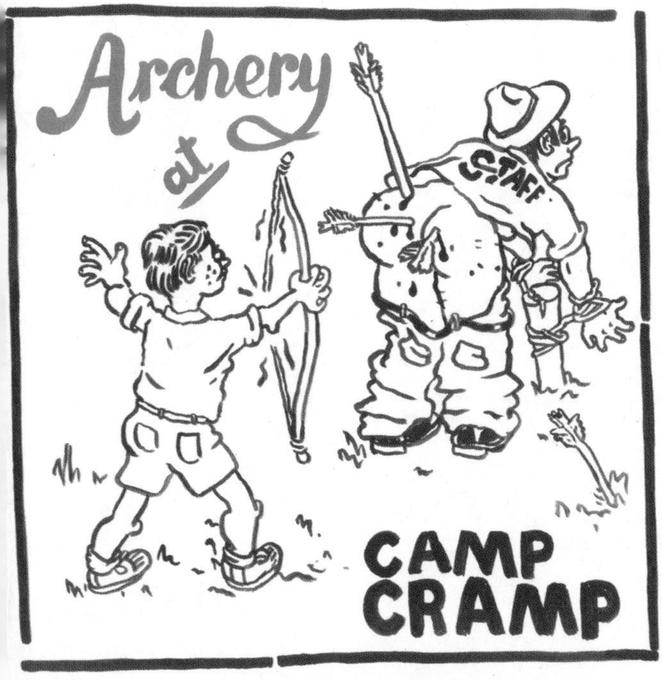
Archery
at
STAFF
CAMP
CRAMP

THE YaMIHere? POOL SCHEDULE

MONDAY	PEE	TOE NAILS	KETTLE OF ERECTIONS	CRAMPS	ALGAE
TUESDAY	ANIMALS	SPUTUM	DEAD & BLOATED	FUN WITH WEIGHTS	LOBSTER BOIL
WEDNESDAY	HAIR BALLS	MUCUS	WATER SNAKES	SURF & TURF	MERMAIDS ONLY
THURSDAY	JUNIOR SINK OR SWIM	BACK & FORTH	FORTH & BACK	CLIFF DIVING	DUNK YOUR JUNK
FRIDAY	SEAFOOD	SWIM RINGS	INFLATABLE GIRLS	PET FISH	STROKE BREAST
SATURDAY	WHALE WATCHING	RUNNING, JUMPING, SCREAMING & SPITTING	DOLPHIN FREE	GET NAKED	FLIPPERS & GILLS
SUNDAY	(CLOSED) PULL THE PLUG & REFILL	(CLOSED) PULL THE PLUG & REFILL	(CLOSED) ADD THE BLEACH & FABRIC SOFTENER	(CLOSED) ADD THE BLEACH & FABRIC SOFTENER	ALL WASHED UP

GET THIS
FREE COMPASS
JUST FOR
SLEEPING WITH
THE EDITOR

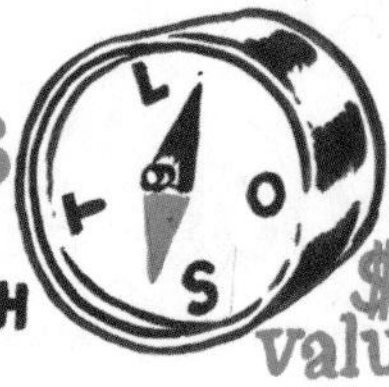
L
O
S
T

A
$12
value

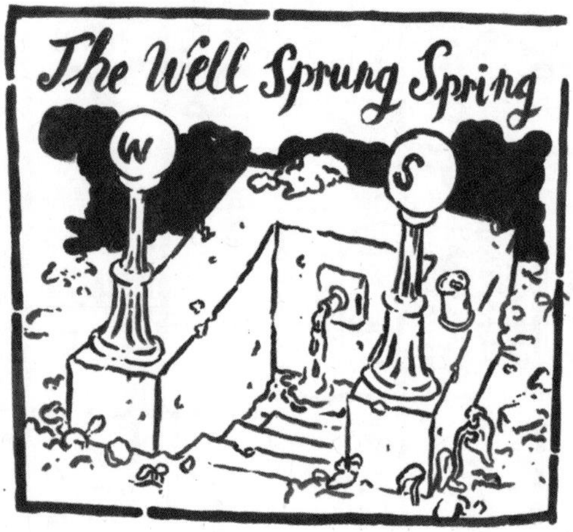
The Well Sprung Spring
W
S

The Ogglefull Museum

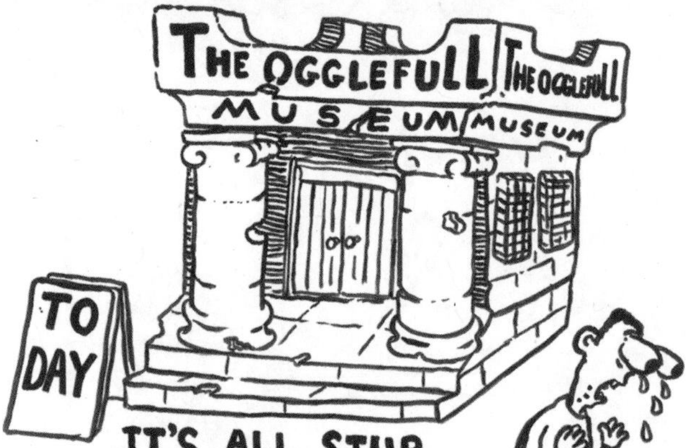
THE OGGLEFULL
MUSEUM
THE OGGLEFULL
MUSEUM
TO
DAY

IT'S ALL STUB
AND NO TICKET

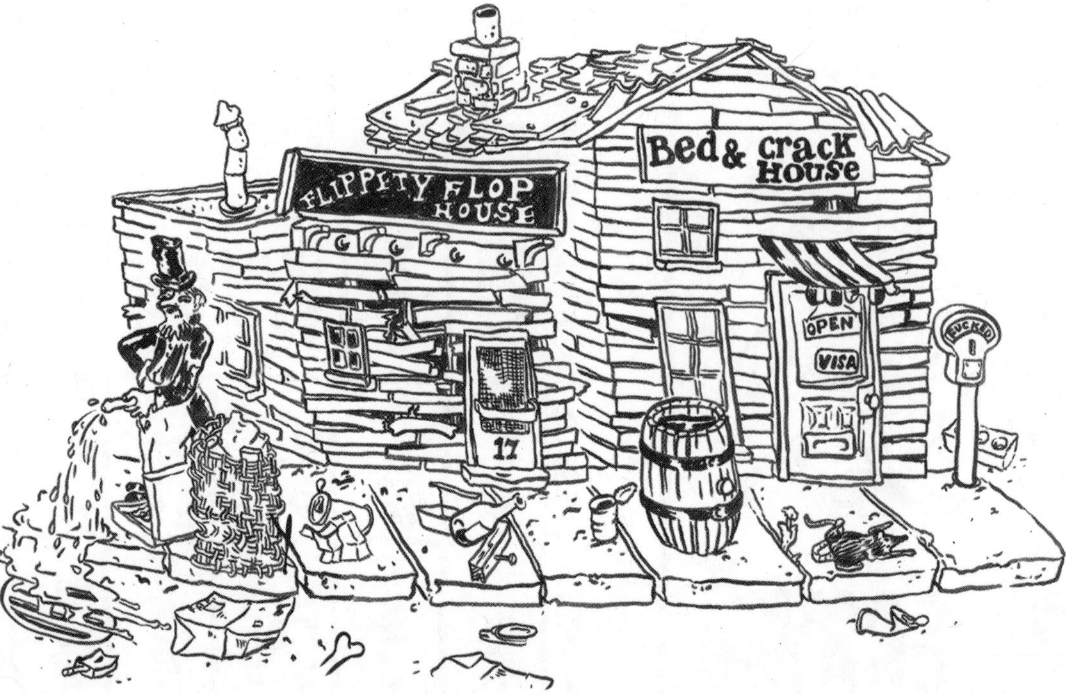
FLIPPETY FLOP
HOUSE
Bed & crack
House
OPEN
VISA
FUCKED
17

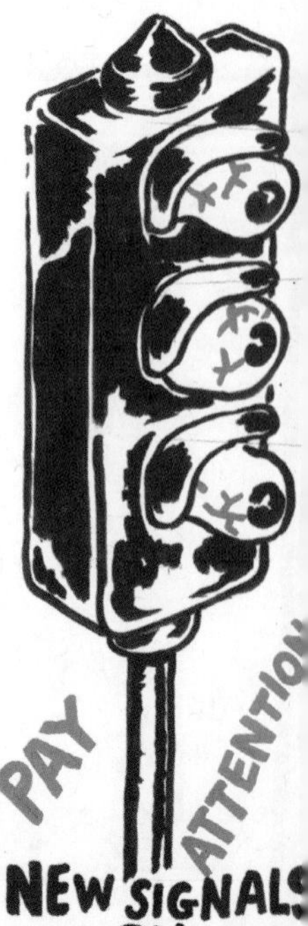
PAY
ATTENTION

NEW SIGNALS
ON
MAIN STREET

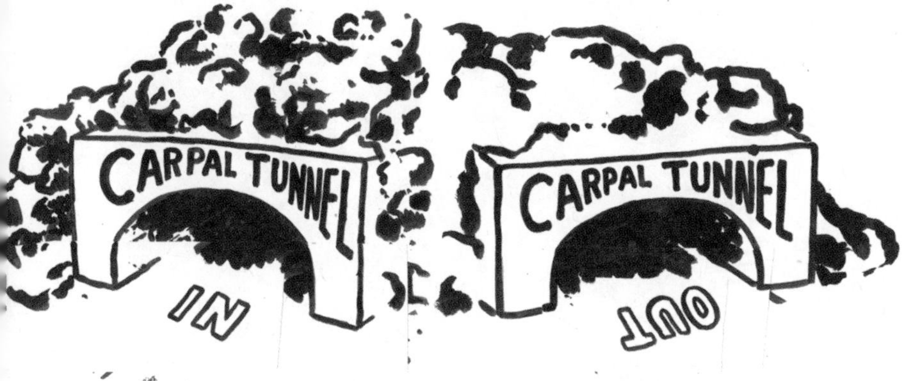
CARPAL TUNNEL
IN
CARPAL TUNNEL
OUT

Two views of Fake Lake's famous Carpal Tunnel. Not for the weak wristed.

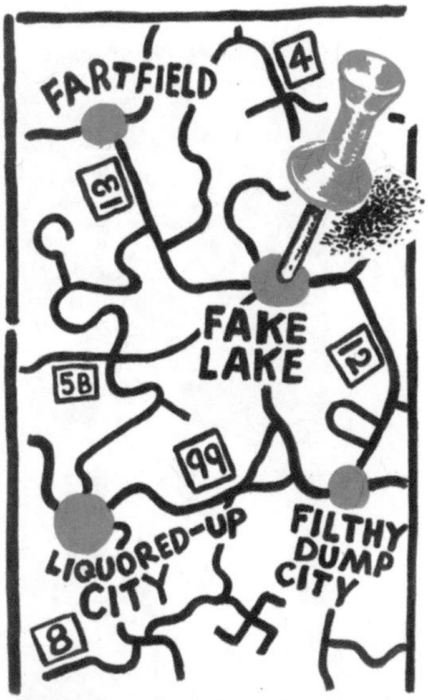
FARTFIELD
4
13
FAKE LAKE
12
5B
99
LIQUORED-UP CITY
FILTHY DUMP CITY
8

FAKE LAKE: WE'RE CLOSE TO EVERYWHERE

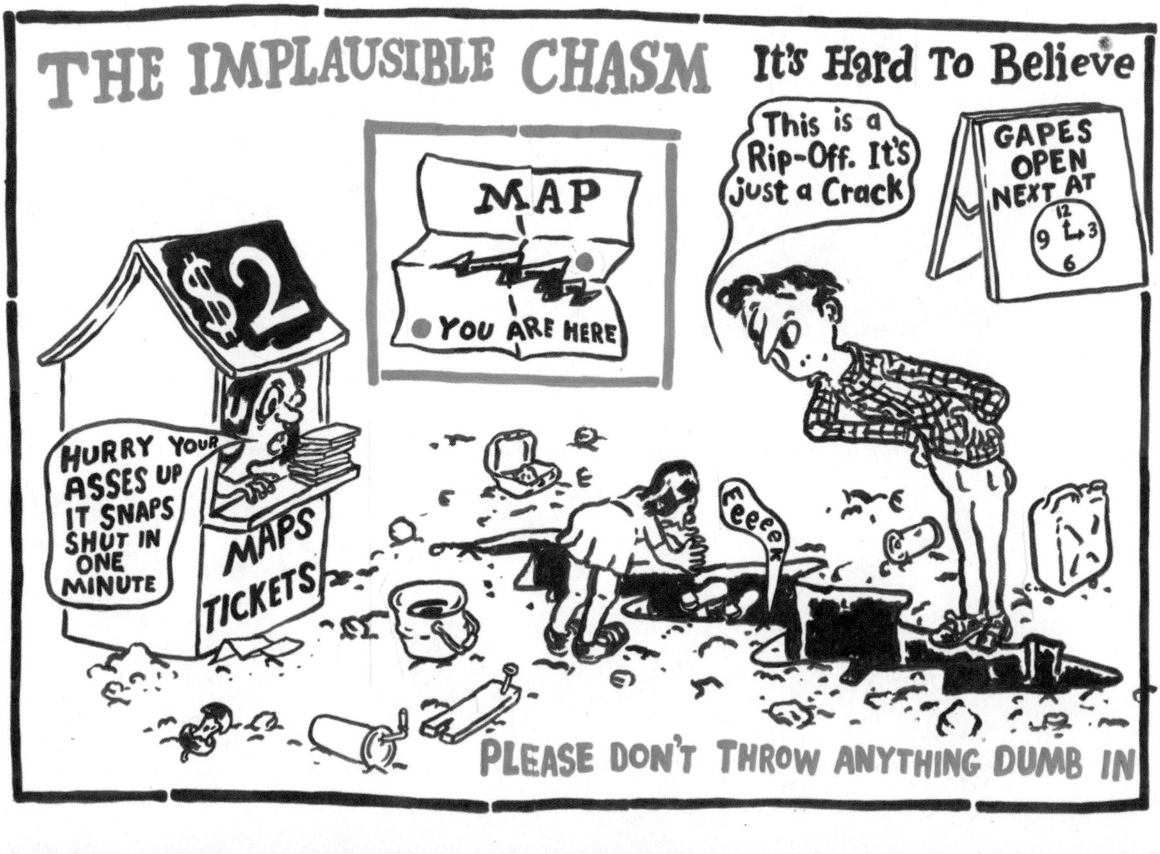
THE IMPLAUSIBLE CHASM It's Hard To Believe
MAP
YOU ARE HERE
$2
HURRY YOUR ASSES UP IT SNAPS SHUT IN ONE MINUTE
MAPS
TICKETS
This is a Rip-Off. It's just a Crack
GAPES OPEN NEXT AT
12 3 6 9
Eeeeek
PLEASE DON'T THROW ANYTHING DUMB IN

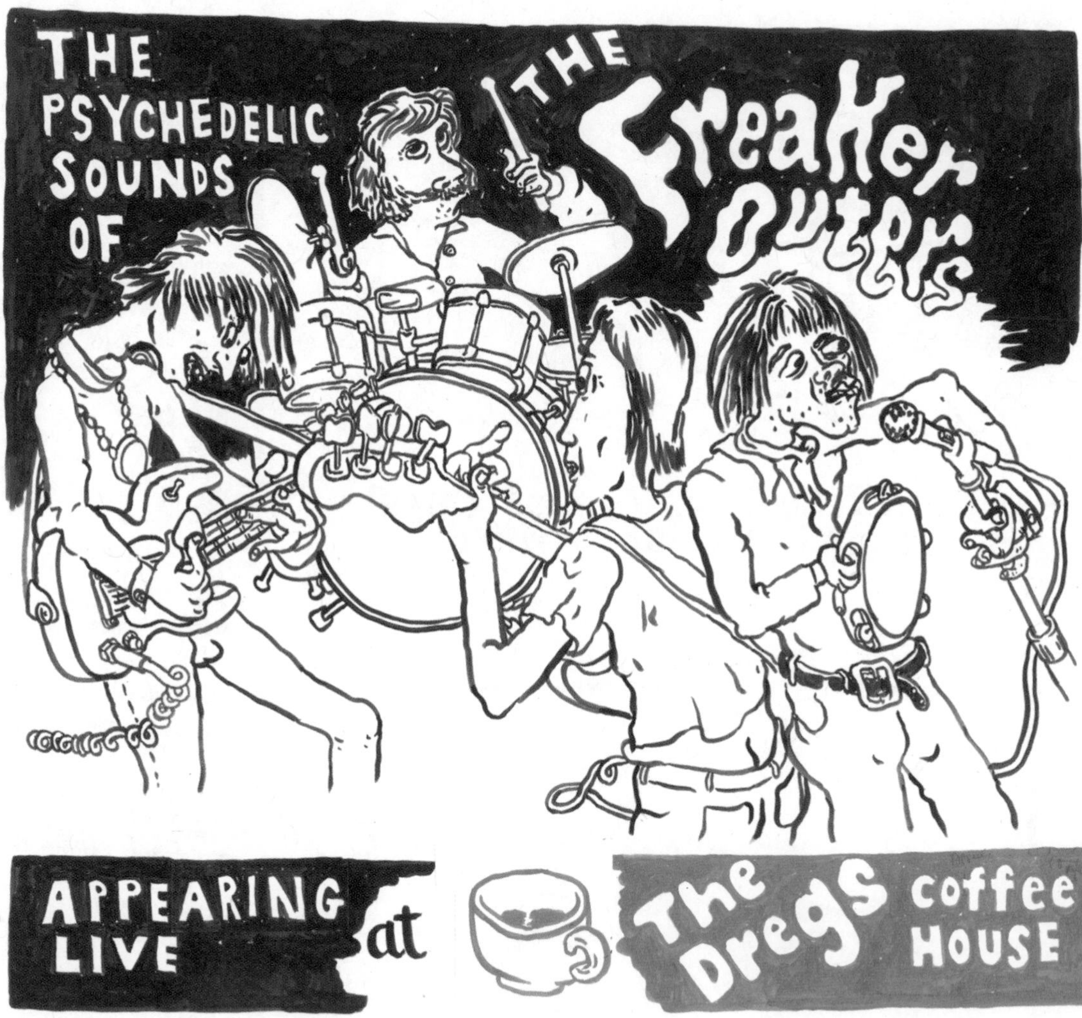
THE PSYCHEDELIC SOUNDS OF
THE Freaker Outers
APPEARING LIVE
at
The Dregs coffee HOUSE

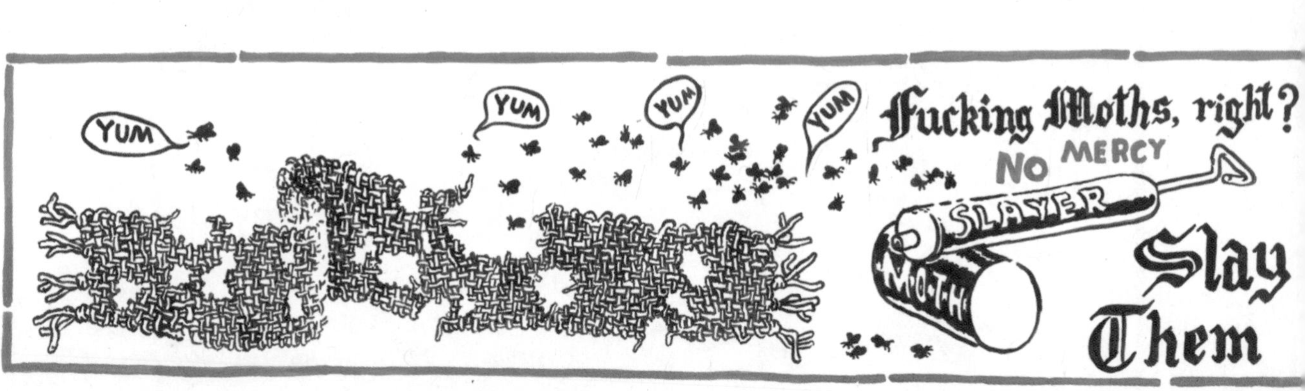
YUM
YUM
YUM
YUM
Fucking Moths, right?
NO MERCY
MOTH SLAYER
Slay Them

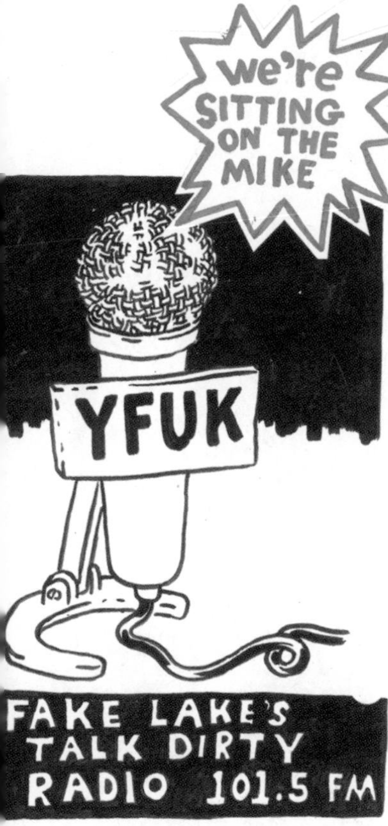
we're SITTING ON THE MIKE
YFUK
FAKE LAKE'S TALK DIRTY RADIO 101.5 FM

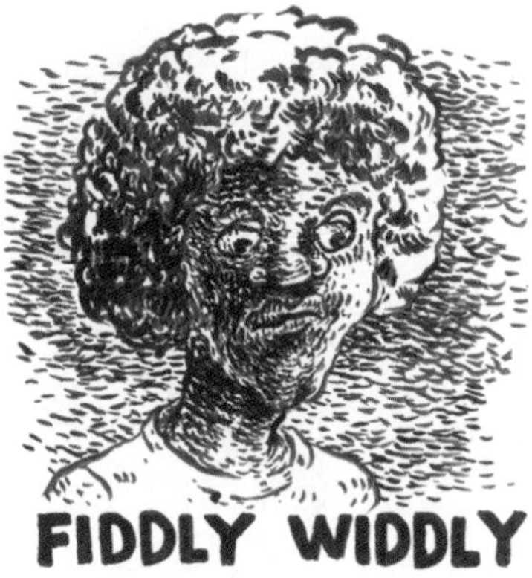
FIDDLY WIDDLY

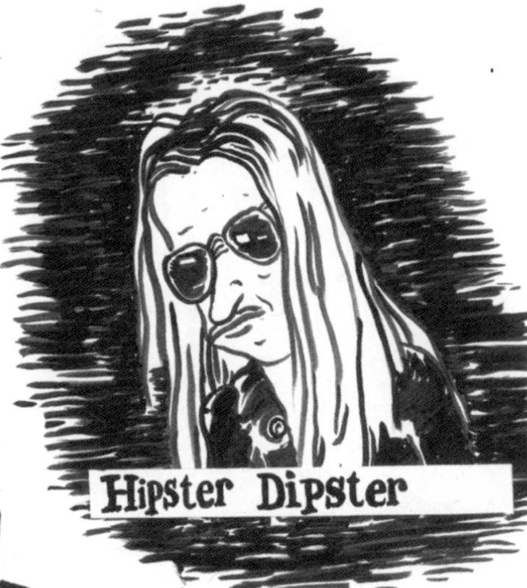
Hipster Dipster

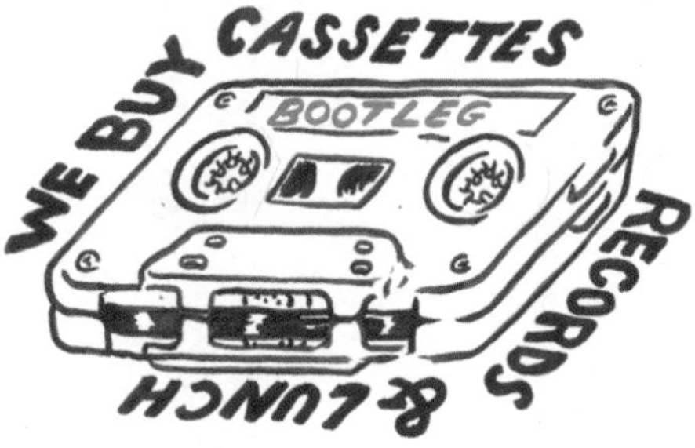
WE BUY CASSETTES
BOOTLEG
RECORDS & LUNCH

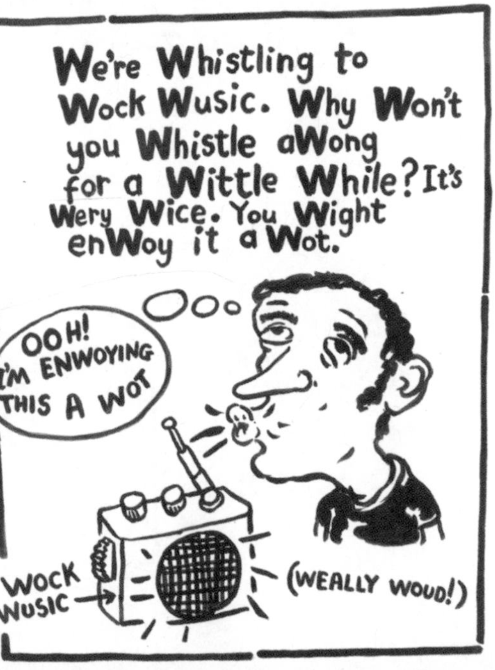
We're Whistling to Wock Wusic. Why Won't you Whistle aWong for a Wittle While? It's Wery Wice. You Wight enWoy it a Wot.
OOH! I'M ENWOYING THIS A WOT
WOCK WUSIC
(WEALLY WOUD!)

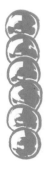

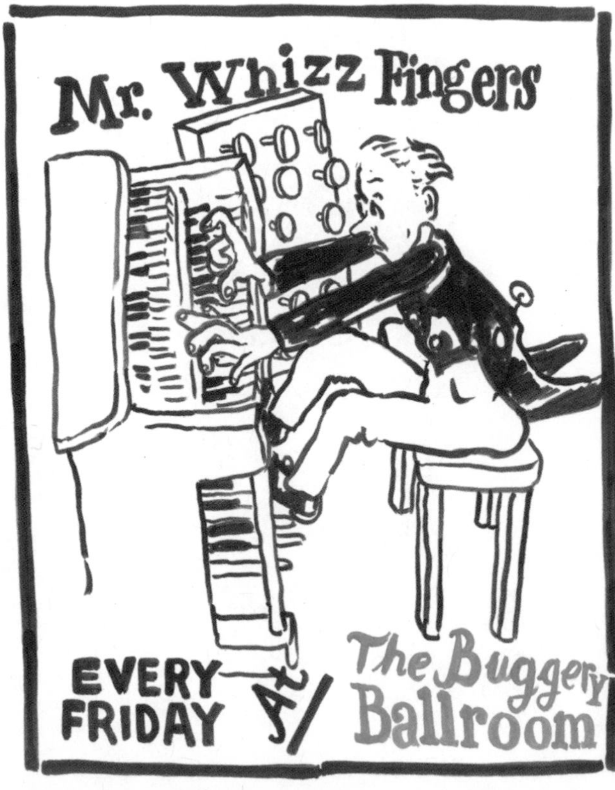
Mr. Whizz Fingers
EVERY FRIDAY At
The Buggery Ballroom

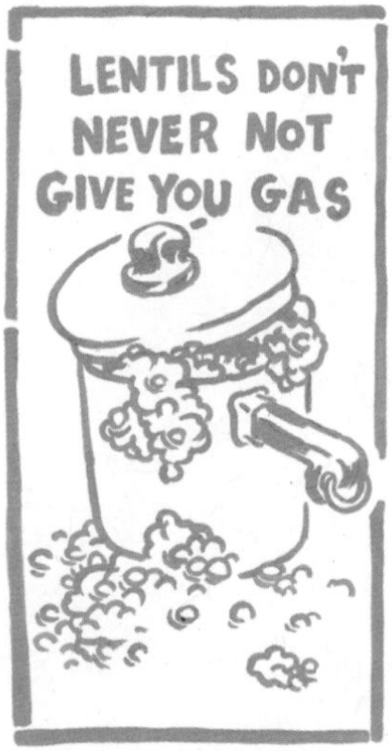
LENTILS DON'T
NEVER NOT
GIVE YOU GAS

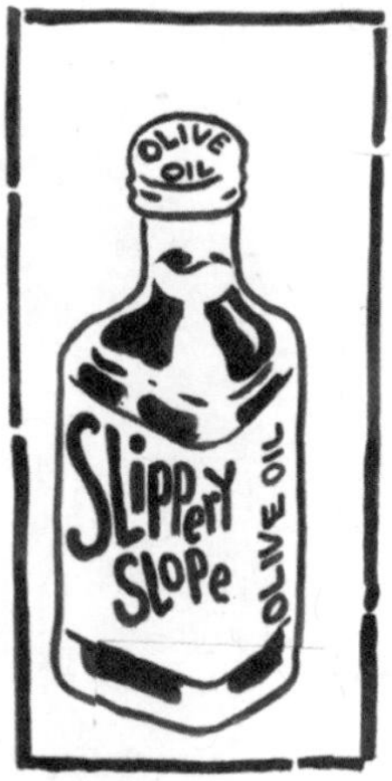
OLIVE OIL
Slippery
Slope
OLIVE OIL

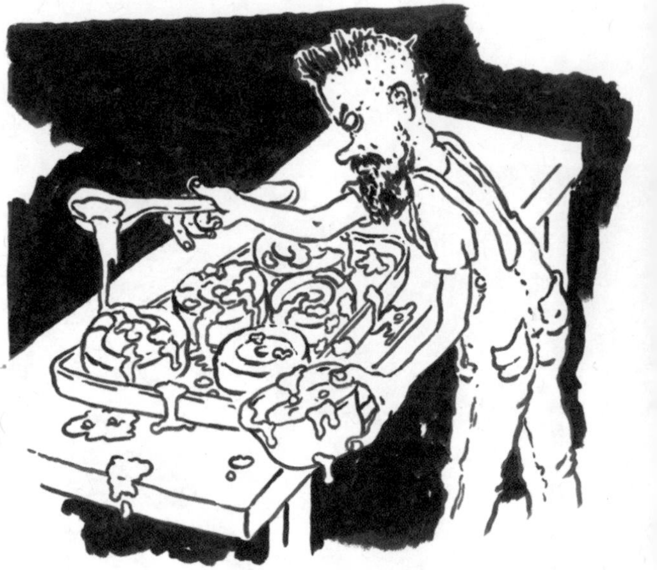

THE STICKY STUFF
Master Patissier Knut Kneadless drizzles the notoriuusly adhesive white icing on a batch of Overly Sticky Buns at the Flakey Bakery. (See next page for our Overly Sticky Buns contest.)

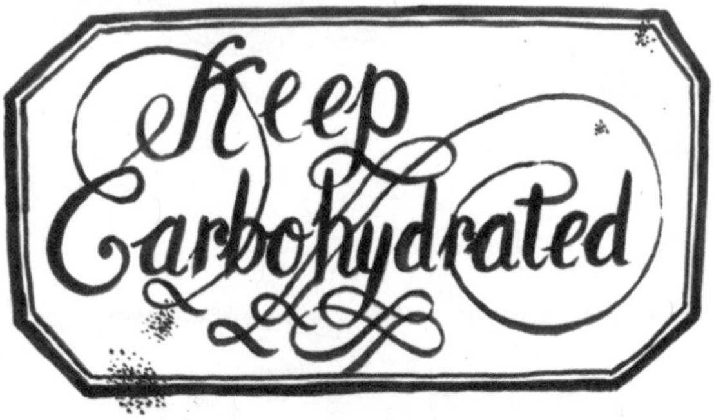
Keep
Carbohydrated

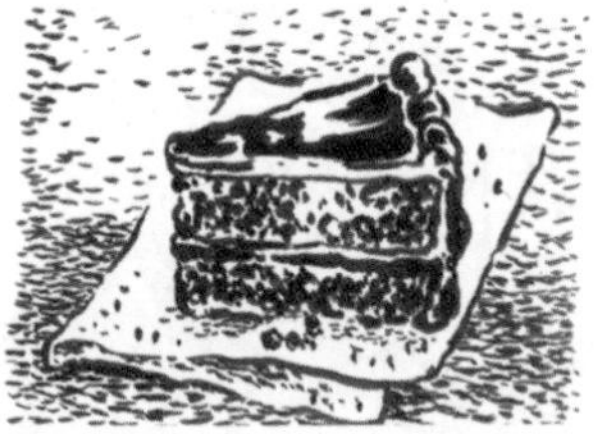

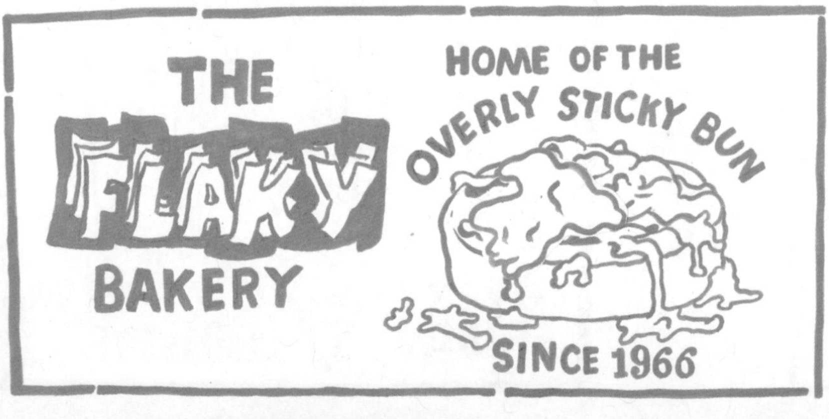
THE
FLAKY
BAKERY
HOME OF THE
OVERLY STICKY BUN
SINCE 1966

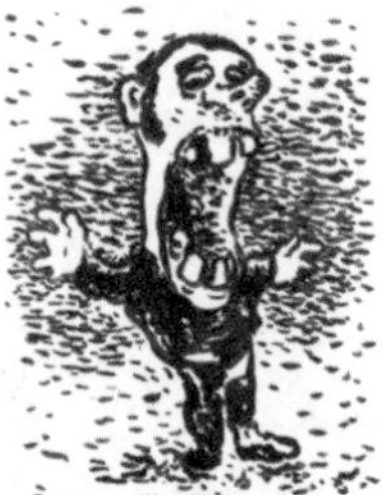

Mr Cake Hole

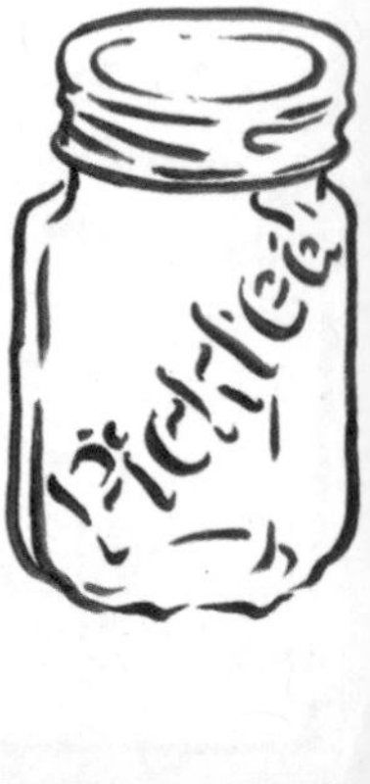
Pickles

THE RESULTS OF THE WHAT CAN YOU DO WITH AN OVERLY STICKY BUN? CONTEST

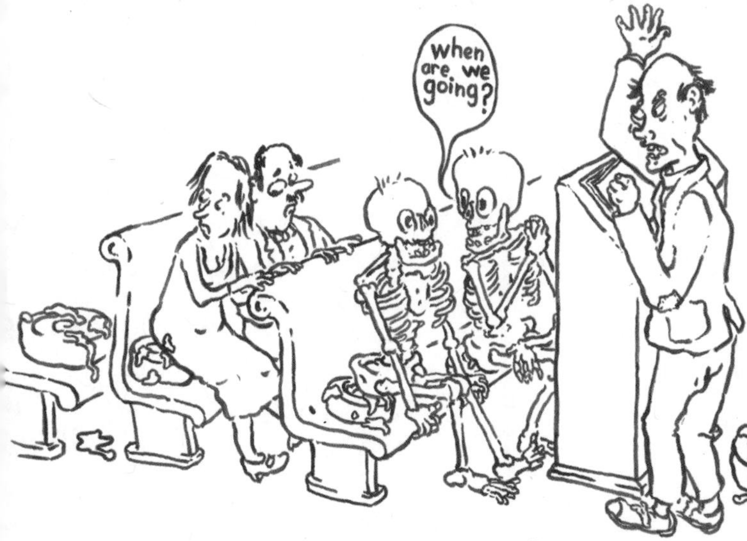
when are we going?

"I use them to Keep my congregation stuck in their seats. They don't budge now."

The REVEREND NEVEREND

(Editor: Beware the overly comfy pew gentle reader!)

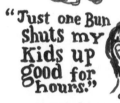

"Just one Bun shuts my Kids up good for hours."

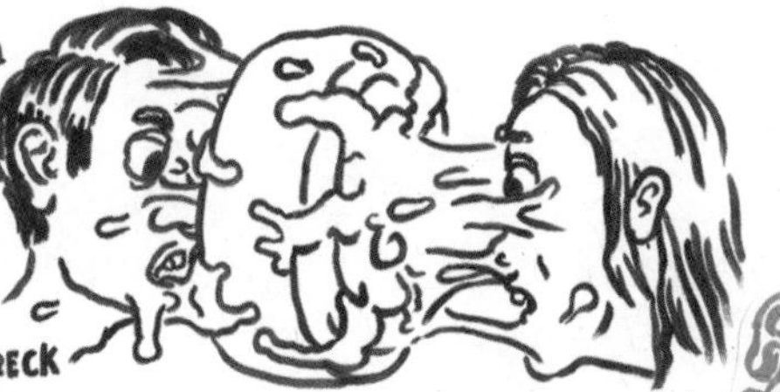

Mrs. HEIDI HOMEWRECK

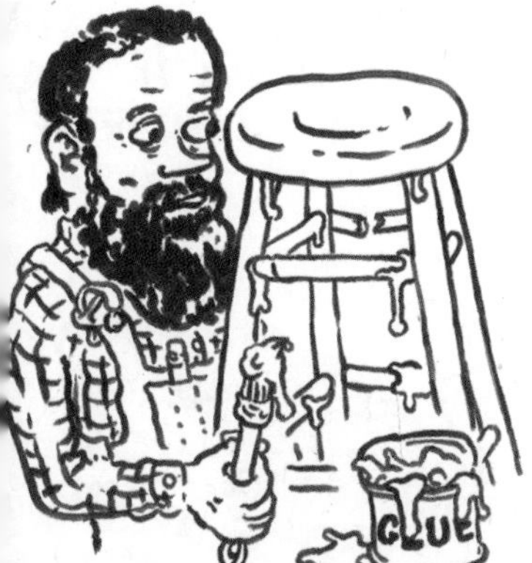
GLUE

"I render them down and use the paste to glue furniture."

SVEN BREADBÖRD

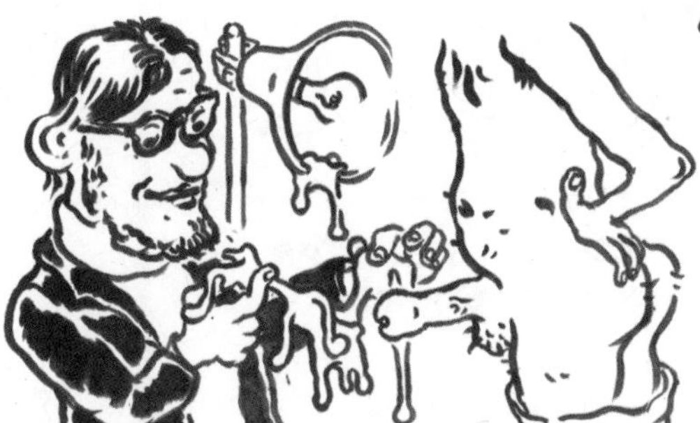

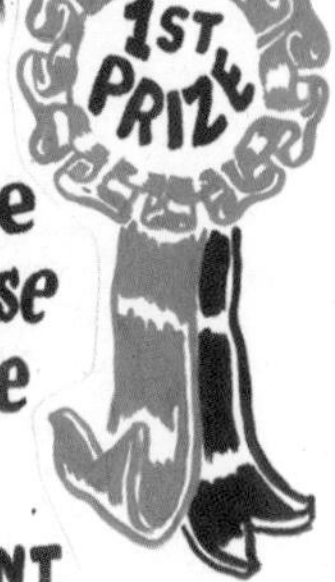
1ST PRIZE

"I peel off the icing and use it to simulate come."

RODNEY WHYFRONT, PORNOGRAPHER

CONGRATULATIONS TO Rodney Whyfront WHO WINS A "Stuck To our Buns" T-SHIRT

SEND YOUR ANSWERS TO NEXT MONTH'S CONTEST TO:
"What can you do with an Overly Sticky Bun? Contest"
C.O. THE FAKE LAKE BOTTOM FEEDER

CHEW WELL

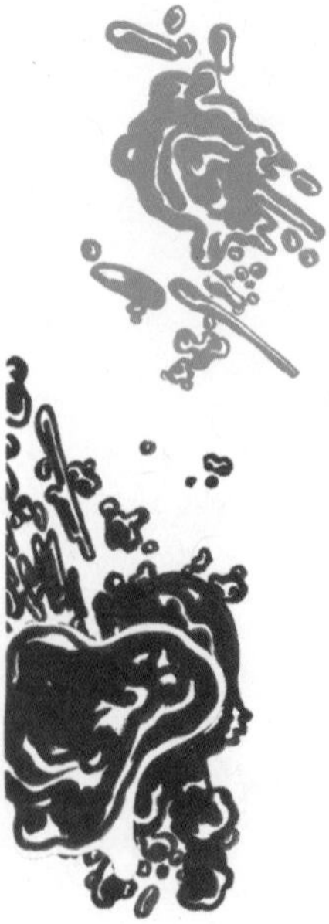

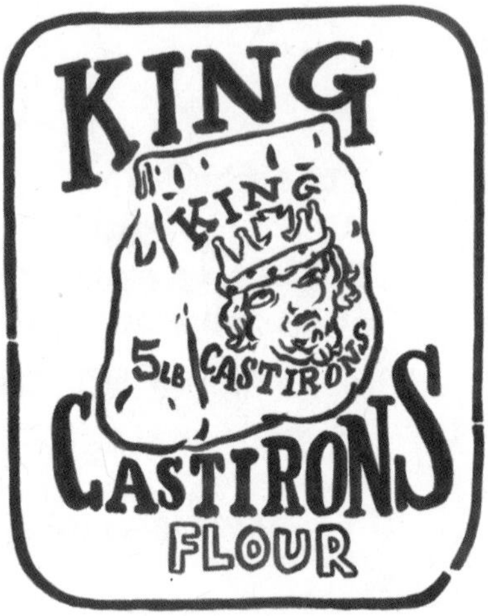
KING
KING
5LB CASTIRONS
CASTIRONS
FLOUR

THE ONE BIG CRUMB CRUMBCAKE

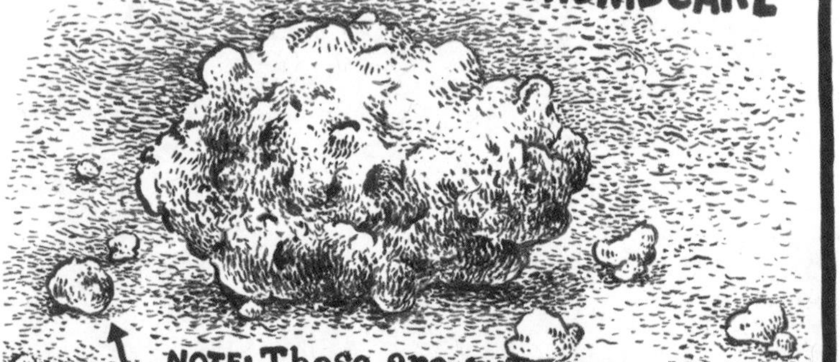

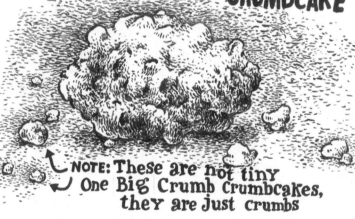

NOTE: These are not tiny One Big Crumb Crumbcakes, they are just crumbs

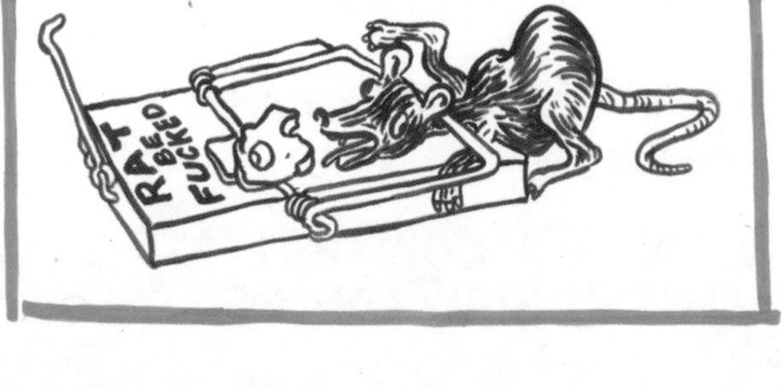
RAT BE FUCKED

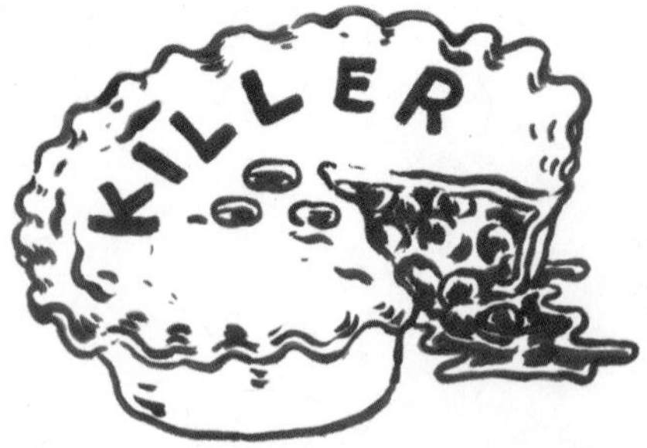
KILLER

Piecrust Deaths

A diabolically tough piecrust was believed responsible for the deaths of three people Sunday. The baker, Mrs. Coughitup Sai "I baked it the way I alway do with King Castiron's pastry Flour. It's not my fault their jaws are made of putty. You gotta chew a pie good if You want it to go down."

Dead Are:

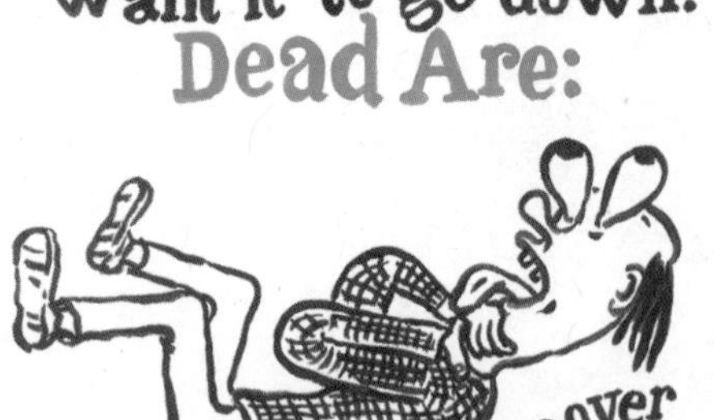

Mr. John Soonover

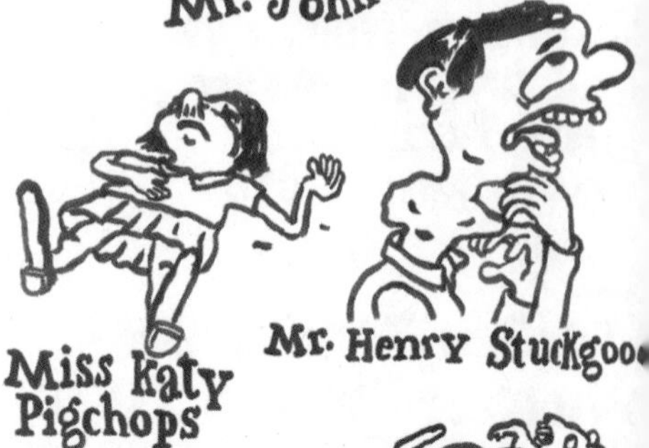

Miss Katy Pigchops

Mr. Henry Stuckgoo

&

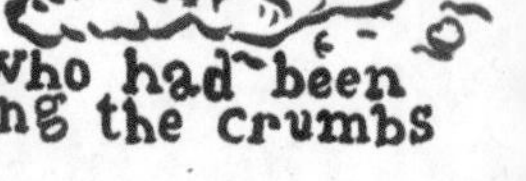

a squirrel who had been eating the crumbs

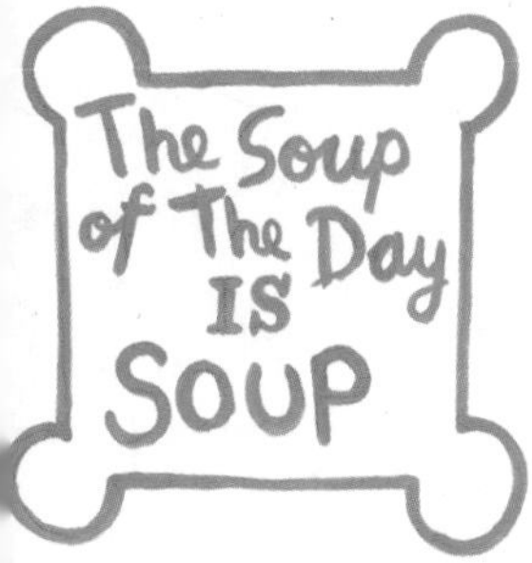
The Soup of The Day IS SOUP

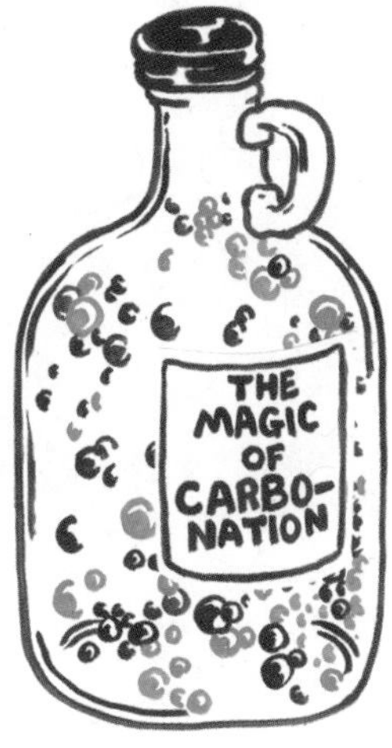
THE MAGIC OF CARBO-NATION

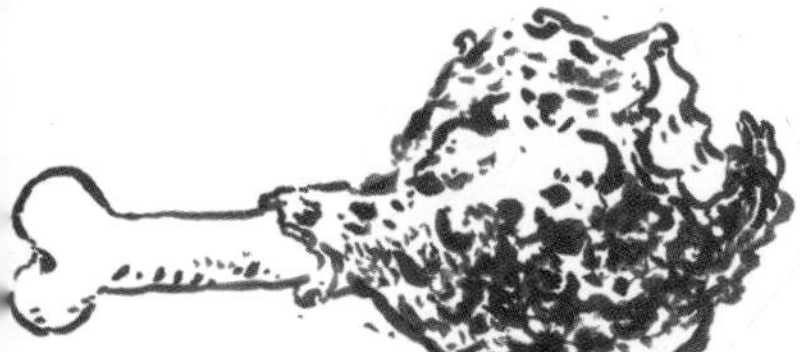

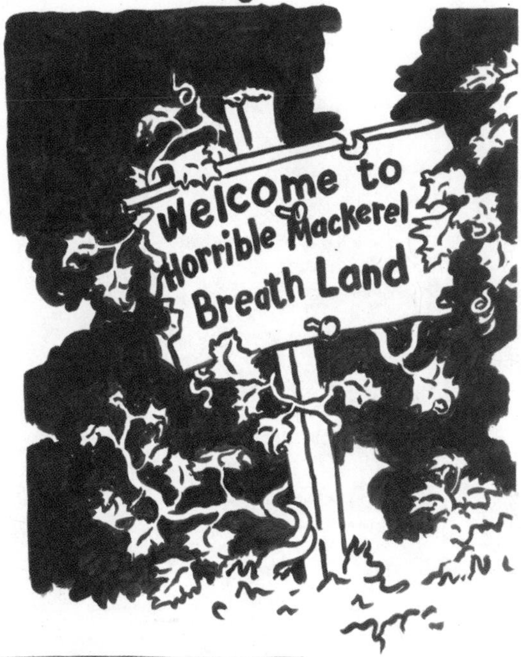
Welcome to Horrible Mackerel Breath Land

FaKing Bacon

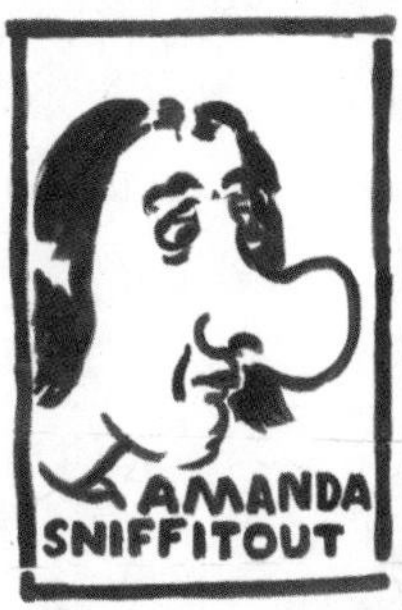
AMANDA SNIFFITOUT

The secret of the Greasy Spoon's famous bacon was discovered this week by our star reporter Amanda Sniffitout. It is indeed cut from a huge job lot of red rubber boots that the Greasy Spoon purchased years ago. The diner maintains that customers prefer it to real back bacon, jokingly referring to it as "surreal back bacon" on account of it's intense red color and marked bounce. (And it's vegetarian friendly to boot! Editor.)

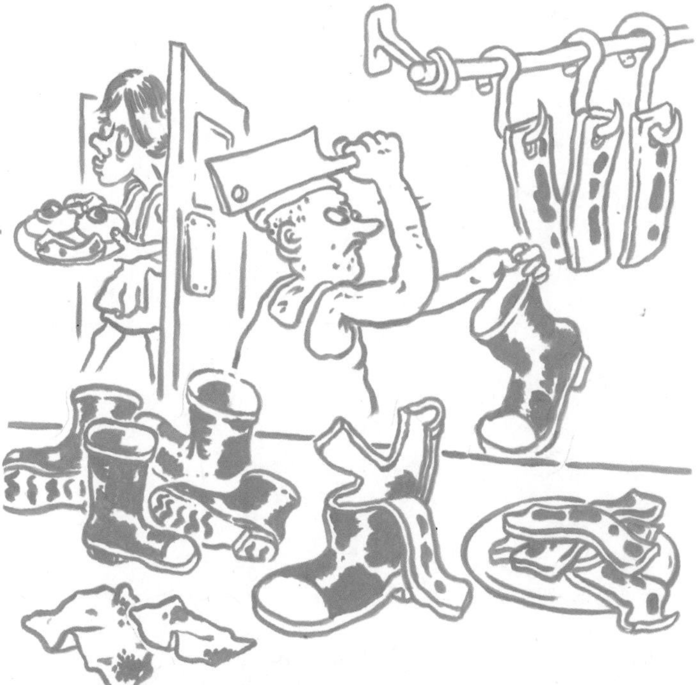

Greasy Spoon chef, Donald Groundround, making bacon

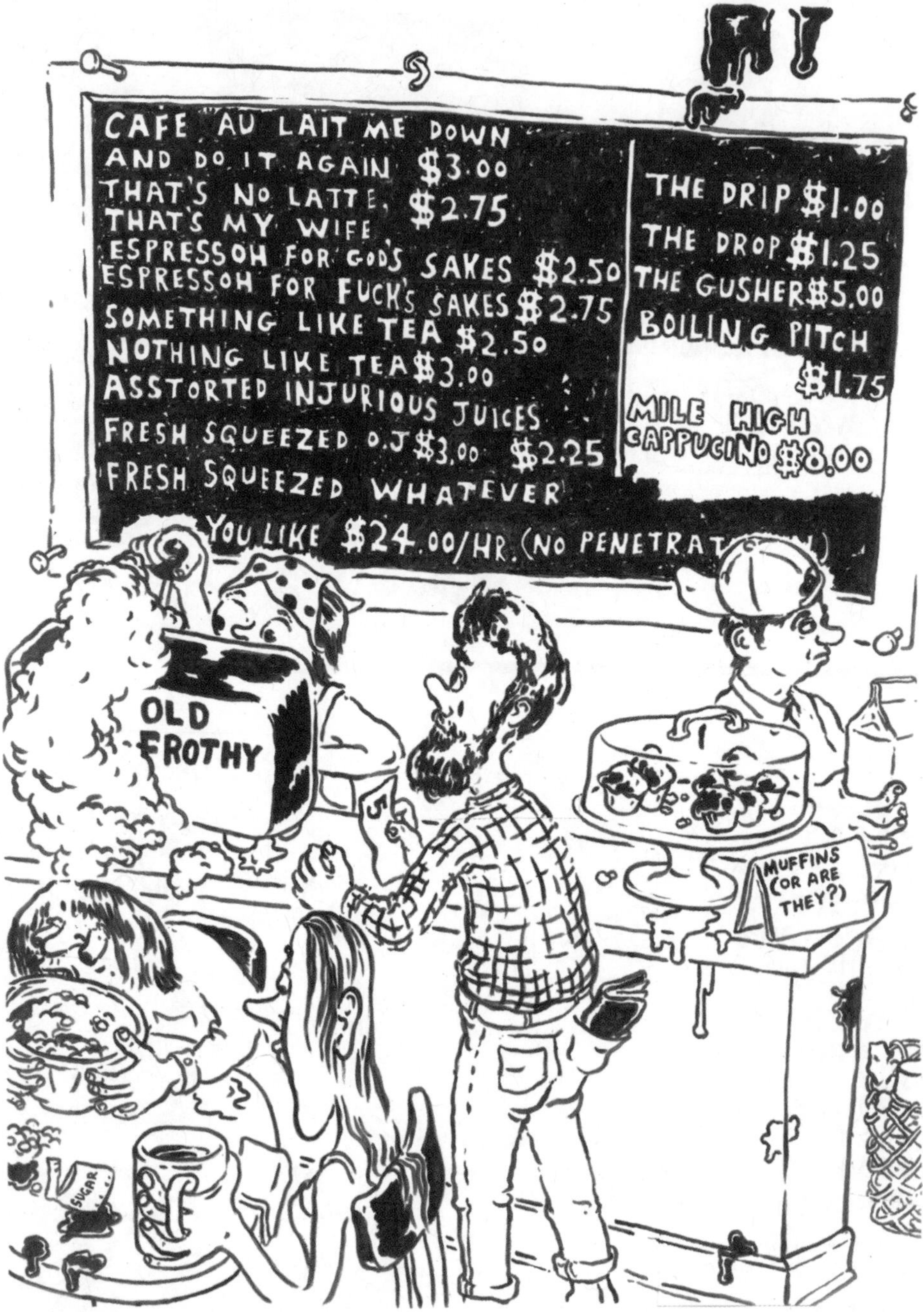
CAFE AU LAIT ME DOWN AND DO IT AGAIN $3.00
THAT'S NO LATTE, THAT'S MY WIFE $2.75
ESPRESSOH FOR GOD'S SAKES $2.50
ESPRESSOH FOR FUCK'S SAKES $2.75
SOMETHING LIKE TEA $2.50
NOTHING LIKE TEA $3.00
ASSTORTED INJURIOUS JUICES
FRESH SQUEEZED O.J $3.00 $2.25
FRESH SQUEEZED WHATEVER YOU LIKE $24.00/HR. (NO PENETRAT
THE DRIP $1.00
THE DROP $1.25
THE GUSHER $5.00
BOILING PITCH $1.75
MILE HIGH CAPPUCINO $8.00
OLD FROTHY
MUFFINS (OR ARE THEY?)
SUGAR

Sue Sludgelover serves up a foamy one to Björn Lawnornament at The Dregs Wednesday afternoon

FULL COVERAGE OF THE DREGS COFFEE SHOP'S SPONSORED EXPEDITION TO ASCEND ~OLD~ FROTHY

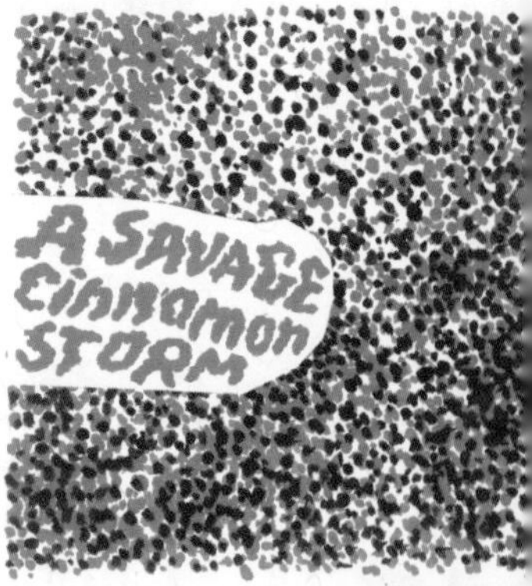
A SAVAGE Cinnamon STORM

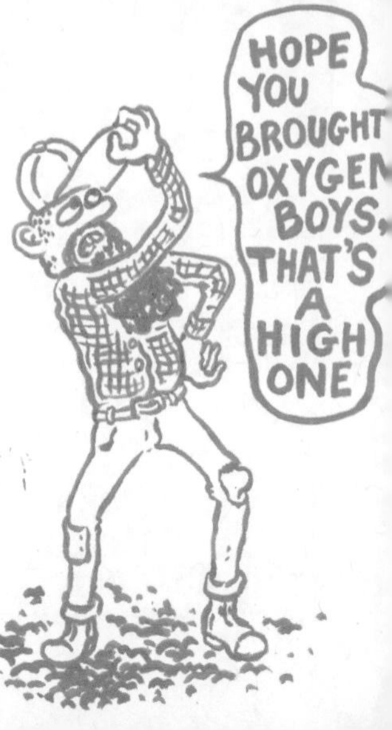
HOPE YOU BROUGHT OXYGEN BOYS, THAT'S A HIGH ONE

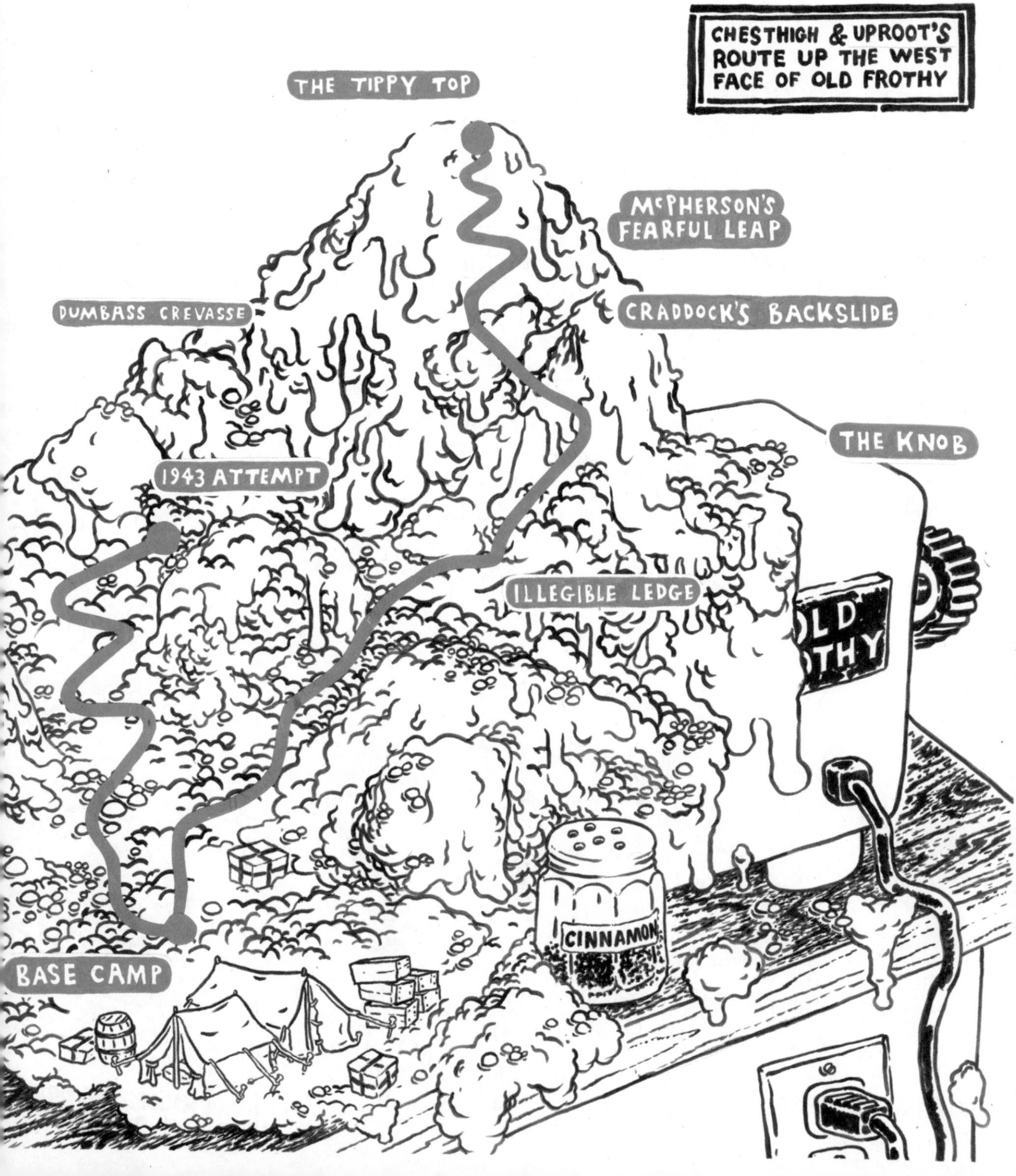
CHESTHIGH & UPROOT'S ROUTE UP THE WEST FACE OF OLD FROTHY
THE TIPPY TOP
McPHERSON'S FEARFUL LEAP
DUMBASS CREVASSE
CRADDOCK'S BACKSLIDE
THE KNOB
1943 ATTEMPT
ILLEGIBLE LEDGE
BASE CAMP
CINNAMON

WHAT TO PACK WHEN YOU'RE CLIMBING A MILE HIGH CAPPUCINO. SIR EDMUND CHESTHIGH'S CHECKLIST

- 2 Packs Very Hard Biscuits
- 2 Packs Much Softer Biscuits
- 1 Pair Very Long Underwear
- 1 Pair Much Shorter Underwear
- 1 Pair positively Miniature Underwear
- 1 Jar Sun-be-gone Cream
- 1 Jar Chafe-chaser Cream
- 1 Tube Never-again Bunion Ointment

- Hand Knit, Polo Neck Bum warmer sweater with matching Hat
- 2 "Good Wacking Tonite" Bivouac Bags
- 3 doz. To Go cups with Lids
- 1 Ice Age Axe
- 1 somewhat Newer Axe
- 2 Pairs Kitten Mittens
- Teeny Weeny Tent
- 1 Rumpus Compass
- Fanny Pack

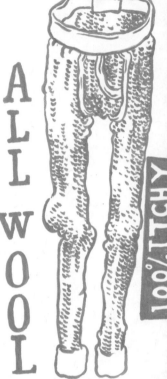

Slackbottom's

ALL WOOL

100% ITCHY

PROFOUNDLY LONG JOHNS

SIR EDMUND CHESTHIGH

> I CANNOT SEE ONE THING SIR EDMUND. WHEN IS THE NEXT CAPPUCINO STOP?

> COURAGE TONSIL. THE FROTH WILL NOT WAIT, IT IS COLLAPSING AS WE SPEAK. WE PUSH ON.

HIS SHERPA GUIDE TONSIL UPROOT

FREE TIBET

IMPERILLED BY DEEP FOAM AT 2000 FEET

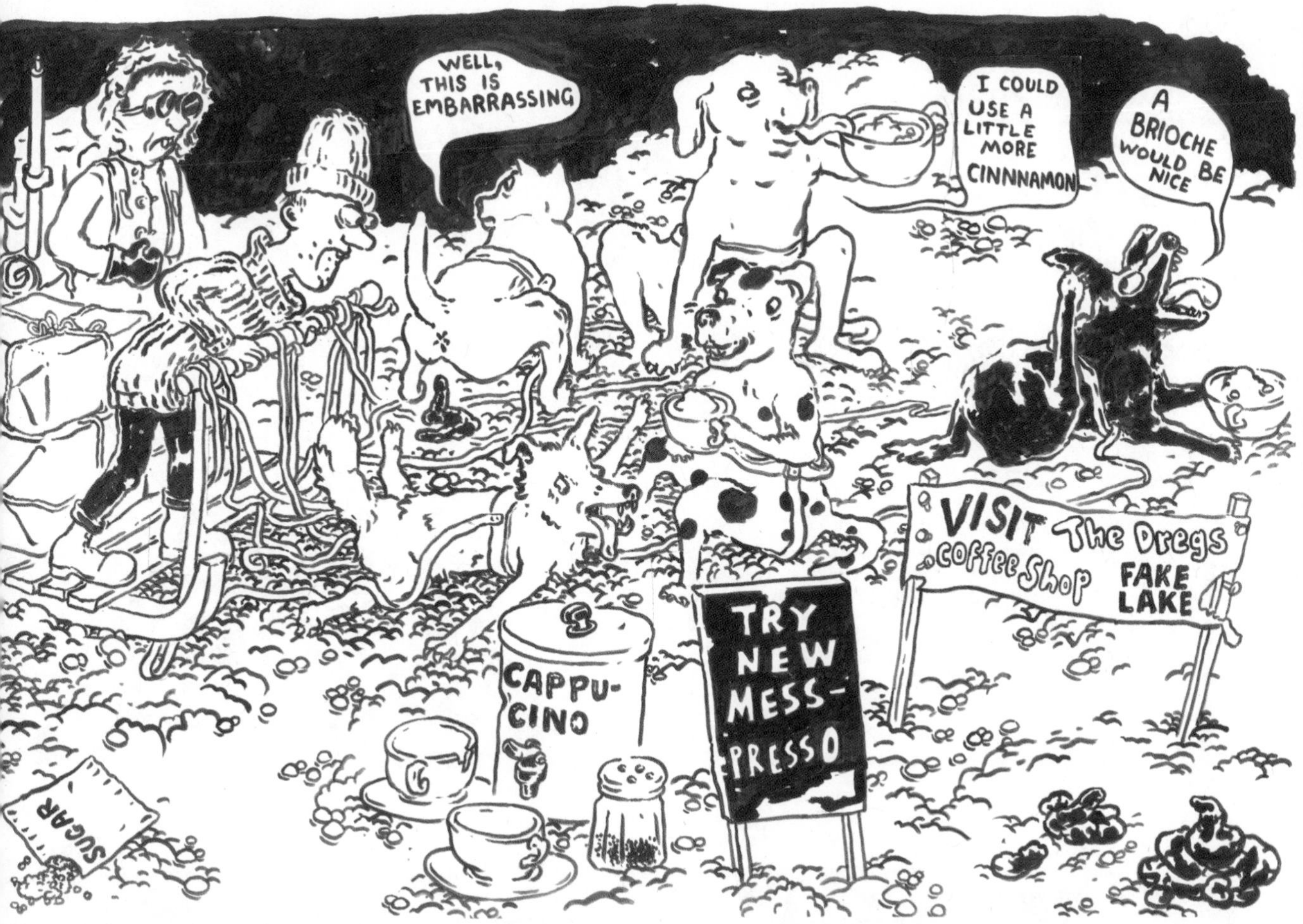
WELL, THIS IS EMBARRASSING
I COULD USE A LITTLE MORE CINNAMON
A BRIOCHE WOULD BE NICE
VISIT The Dregs coffee Shop
FAKE LAKE
TRY NEW MESS-PRESSO
CAPPU-CINO
SUGAR

A LITTLE TROUBLE WITH THE DOGSLED TEAM APPROACHING THE TREACHEROUS DUMBASS CREVASSE

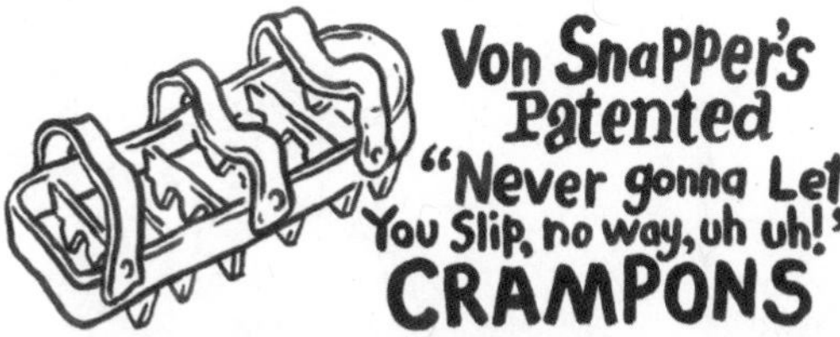
Von Snapper's
Patented
"Never gonna Let You Slip, no way, uh uh!"
CRAMPONS

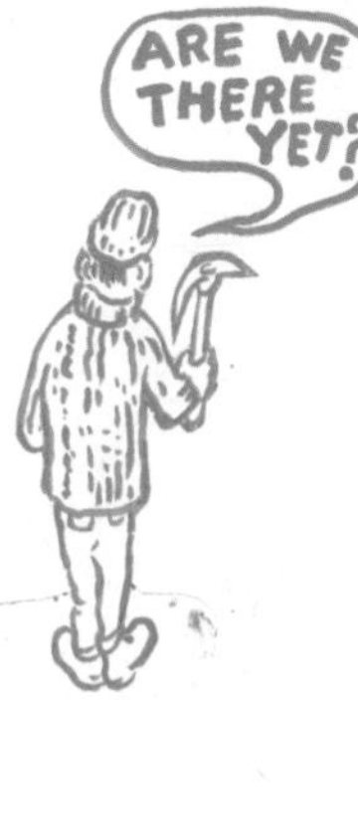
ARE WE THERE YET?

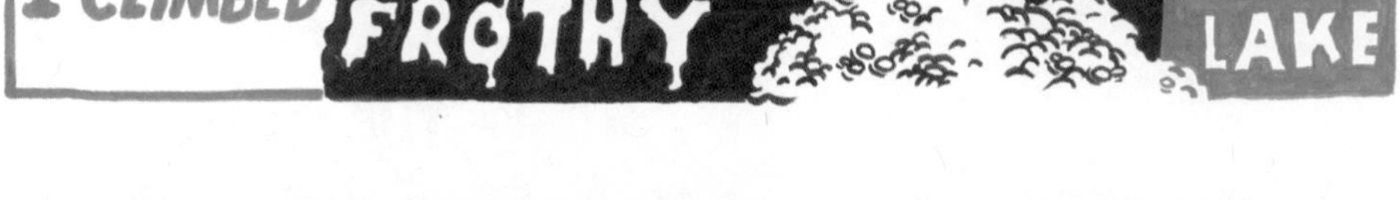
I CLIMBED
OLD FROTHY
FAKE LAKE

TODAY'S STAR POEM

Frisket, frisket,
I've got a biscuit,

Fiasco, fiasco,
I've got an asshole.

Congratulations to
Miss Linda Splitlip
Age 9½

peanut

Nevr Smudge

HEY KIDS, GROW UP!

POETRY CORNER

I LIKE

I like Olives,
I like glue,
I like figs,
And fuckheads too.

POETRY

SUCKS

STAY IN THE LINES YOU LITTLE BASTARDS. I'M FREAKING OUT HERE

COLOR IN TRIPPY THE CLOWN. TRY TO STAY IN THE LINES.

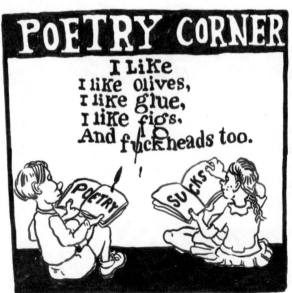

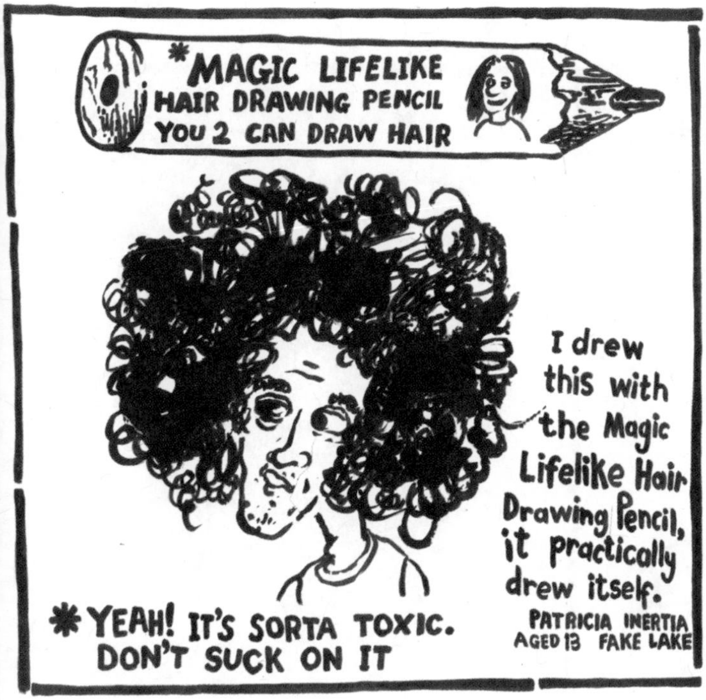
*MAGIC LIFELIKE
HAIR DRAWING PENCIL
YOU 2 CAN DRAW HAIR
I drew this with the Magic Lifelike Hair Drawing Pencil, it practically drew itself.
PATRICIA INERTIA
AGED 13 FAKE LAKE
*YEAH! IT'S SORTA TOXIC. DON'T SUCK ON IT

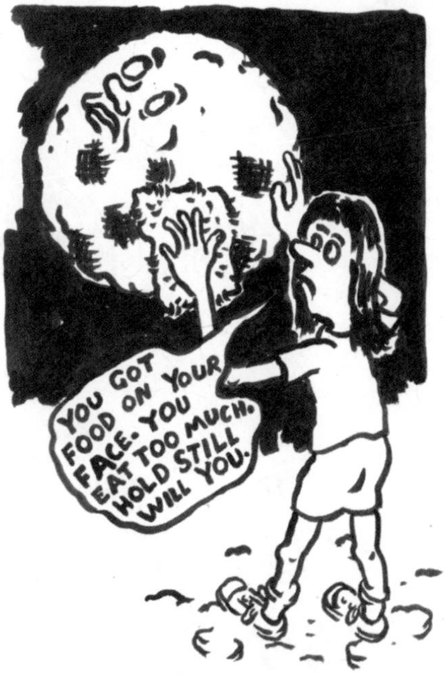
YOU GOT FOOD ON YOUR FACE. YOU EAT TOO MUCH. HOLD STILL WILL YOU.

Lonely Planet,
Spinning in space,
How I'd like to,
Wipe your face.

SAUCERS
&
sorcerers
=
GROCERS
&
GROSSOUTERERS

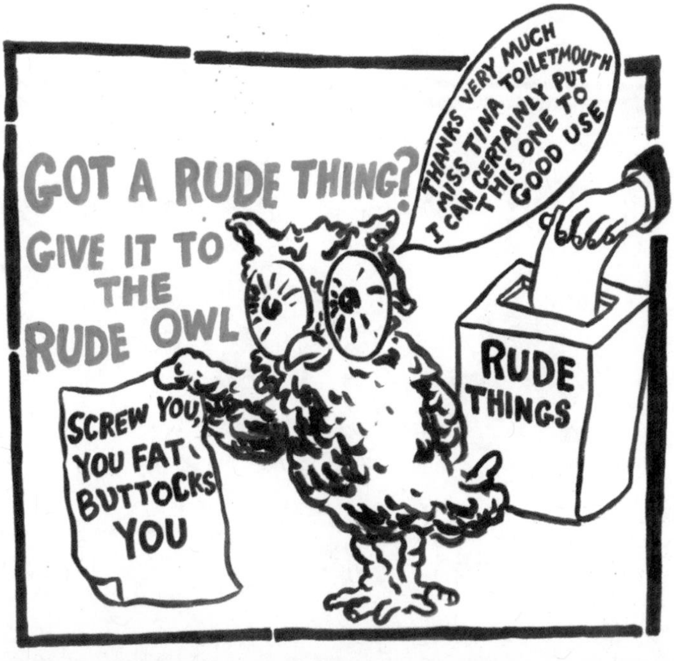
GOT A RUDE THING?
GIVE IT TO THE RUDE OWL
THANKS VERY MUCH MISS TINA TOILETMOUTH I CAN CERTAINLY PUT THIS ONE TO GOOD USE
SCREW YOU, YOU FAT BUTTOCKS YOU
RUDE THINGS

IT'S TUESDAY! IT'S TUESDAY!

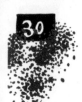

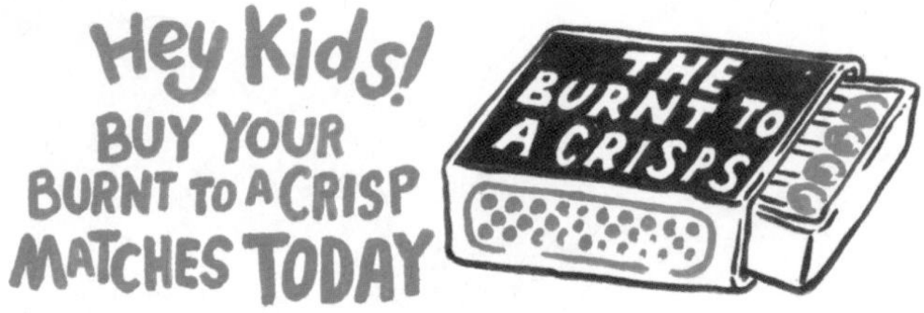
Hey Kids!
BUY YOUR
BURNT TO A CRISP
MATCHES TODAY
THE BURNT TO A CRISPS

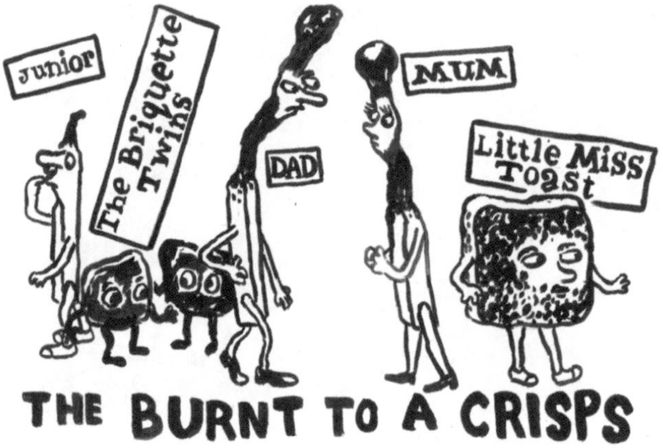
Junior
The Briquette Twins
DAD
MUM
Little Miss Toast
THE BURNT TO A CRISPS

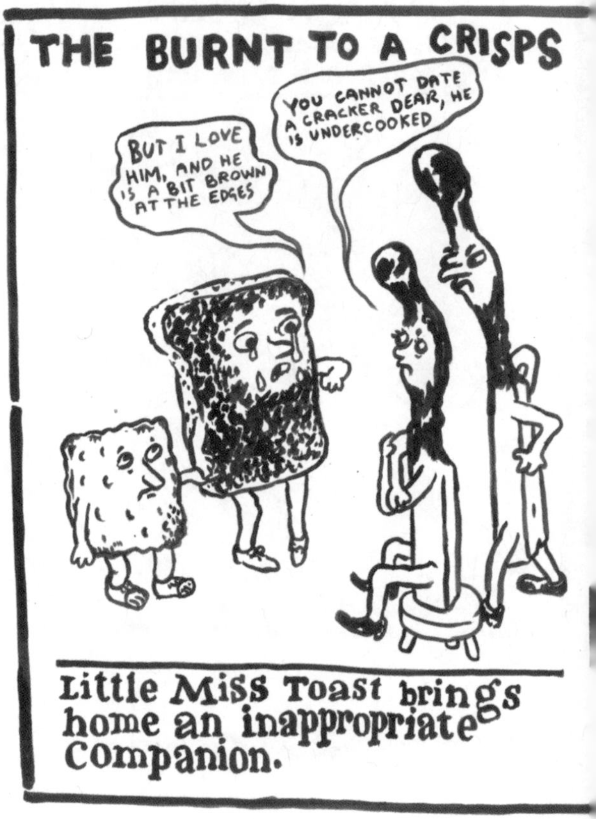
THE BURNT TO A CRISPS
BUT I LOVE HIM, AND HE IS A BIT BROWN AT THE EDGES
YOU CANNOT DATE A CRACKER DEAR, HE IS UNDERCOOKED
Little Miss Toast brings home an inappropriate Companion.

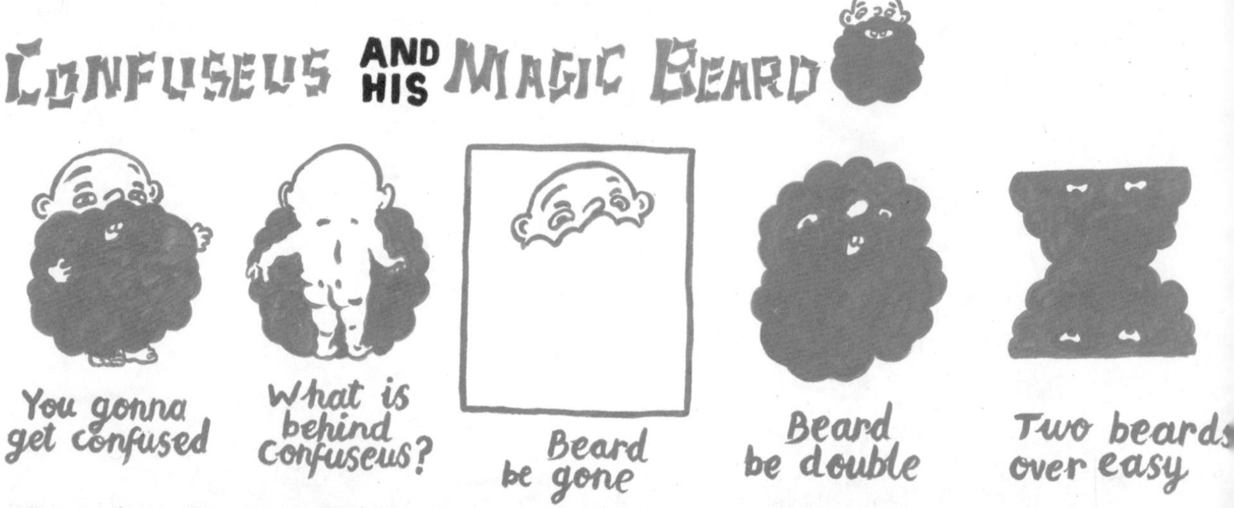
CONFUSEUS AND HIS MAGIC BEARD
You gonna get confused
What is behind confuseus?
Beard be gone
Beard be double
Two beards over easy

"this place is smokin'"

"got any good soot?"

The Briquette Twins sneak into the Hibachi Club.

Buttered Against Her Will

GOINGS ON

Wednesday around lunchtime, Little Miss Toast was ravaged by a blunt knife that forcibly spread butter on her. Her father, Mr. Burnt to A Crisp, alerted by his daughter's cries, confronted the miscreant utensil who fled back to the safety of the cutlery drawer. "It's just not right" said Little Miss Toast "I'm not just a common, ordinary piece of toast, I'm Burnt To A Crisp, we don't do butter."

FOLLOW CONFUSEUS (IF YOU CAN) EVERY TUESDAY IN THE BOTTOM FEEDER

oh!......

oh! oh!....

oh! oh! oh!...

oh! oh! oh! oh!..

oh! Fuck!

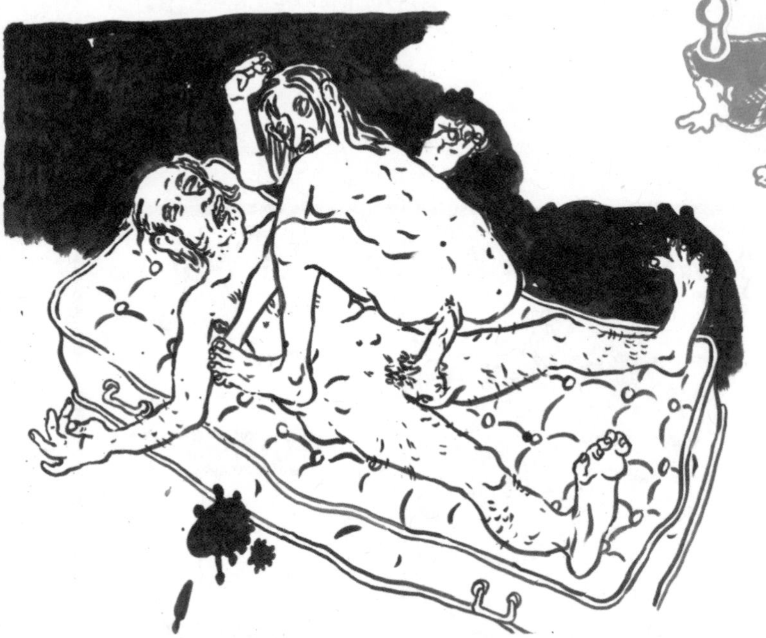

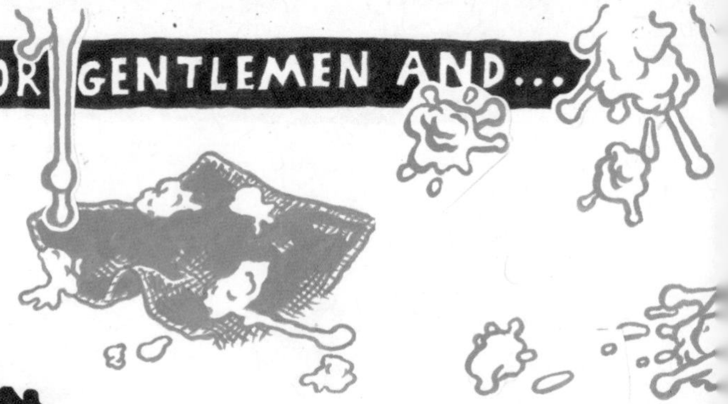

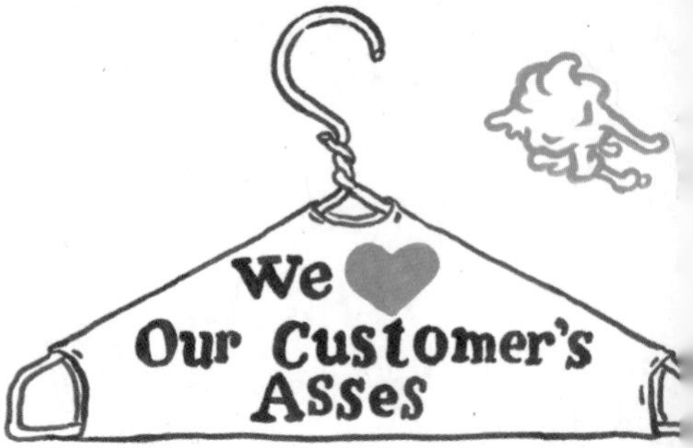
We ♥
Our Customer's
Asses

YOUR MORNING *Smut*

Miss Virginia Whinnyer takes the highroad over Mr. Peter Petersout

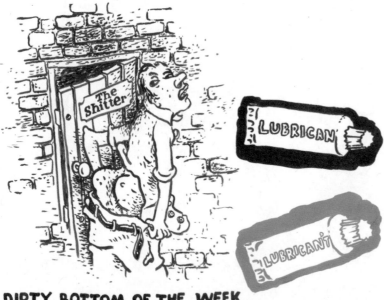

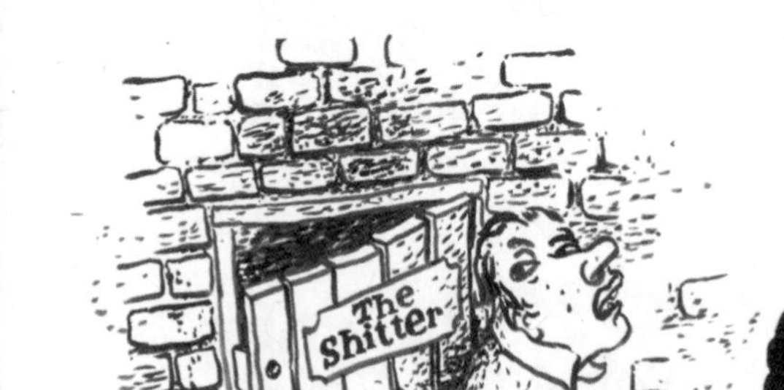
The Shitter

DIRTY BOTTOM OF THE WEEK

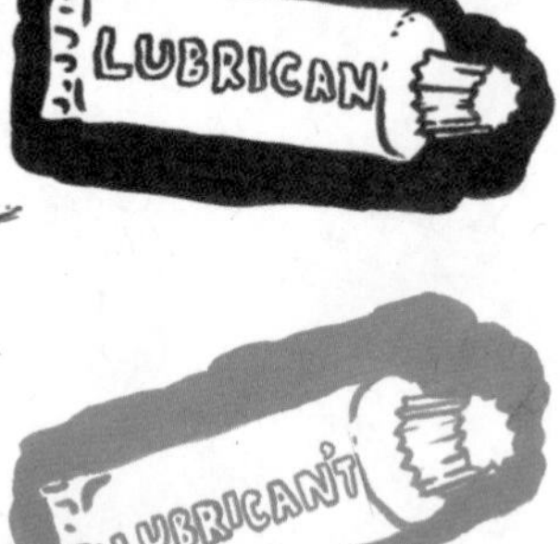
LUBRICAN
LUBRICAN'T

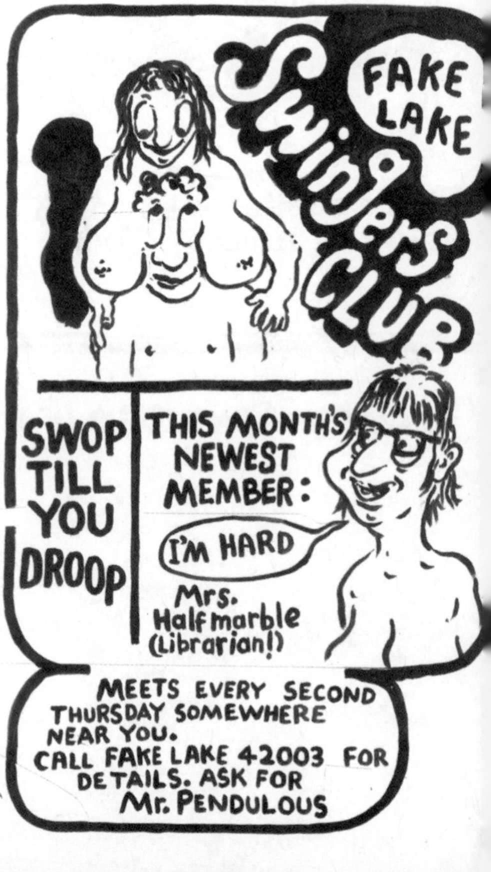
FAKE LAKE
Swingers CLUB
SWOP TILL YOU DROOP
THIS MONTH'S NEWEST MEMBER:
I'M HARD
Mrs. Halfmarble (Librarian!)
MEETS EVERY SECOND THURSDAY SOMEWHERE NEAR YOU.
CALL FAKE LAKE 42003 FOR DETAILS. ASK FOR Mr. PENDULOUS

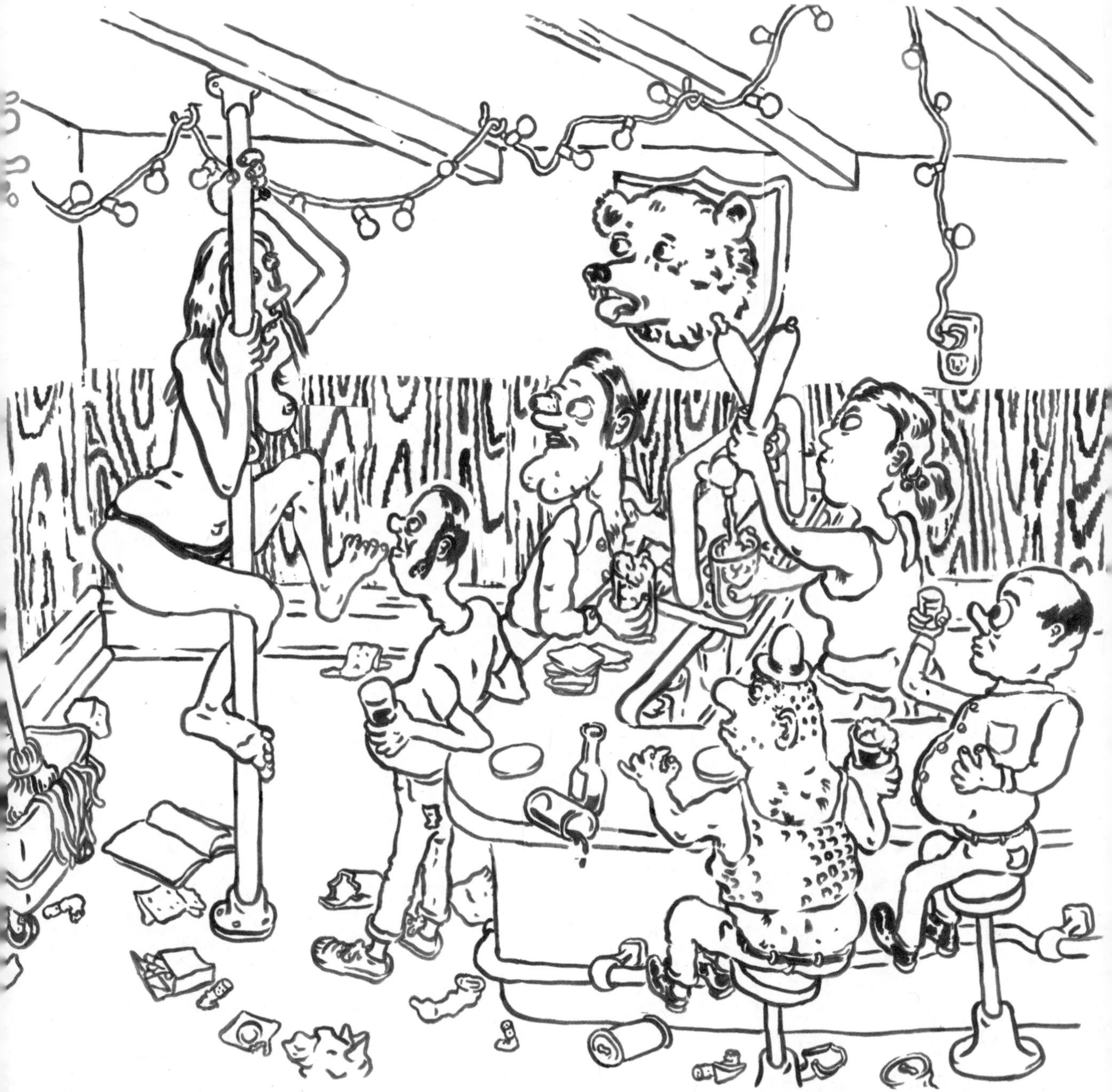

Patrons of the Polished By Bums Tavern get a ast look at Sarahbeth lipslide's Performance n Wednesday night. Miss Slipslide is giving up the pole to marry Mr. Witold Stiffski. "I don't look at it as quitting," said Sarahbeth "more like trading one pole for another." Editor's note: Mr. Stiffski is Polish, apparently.

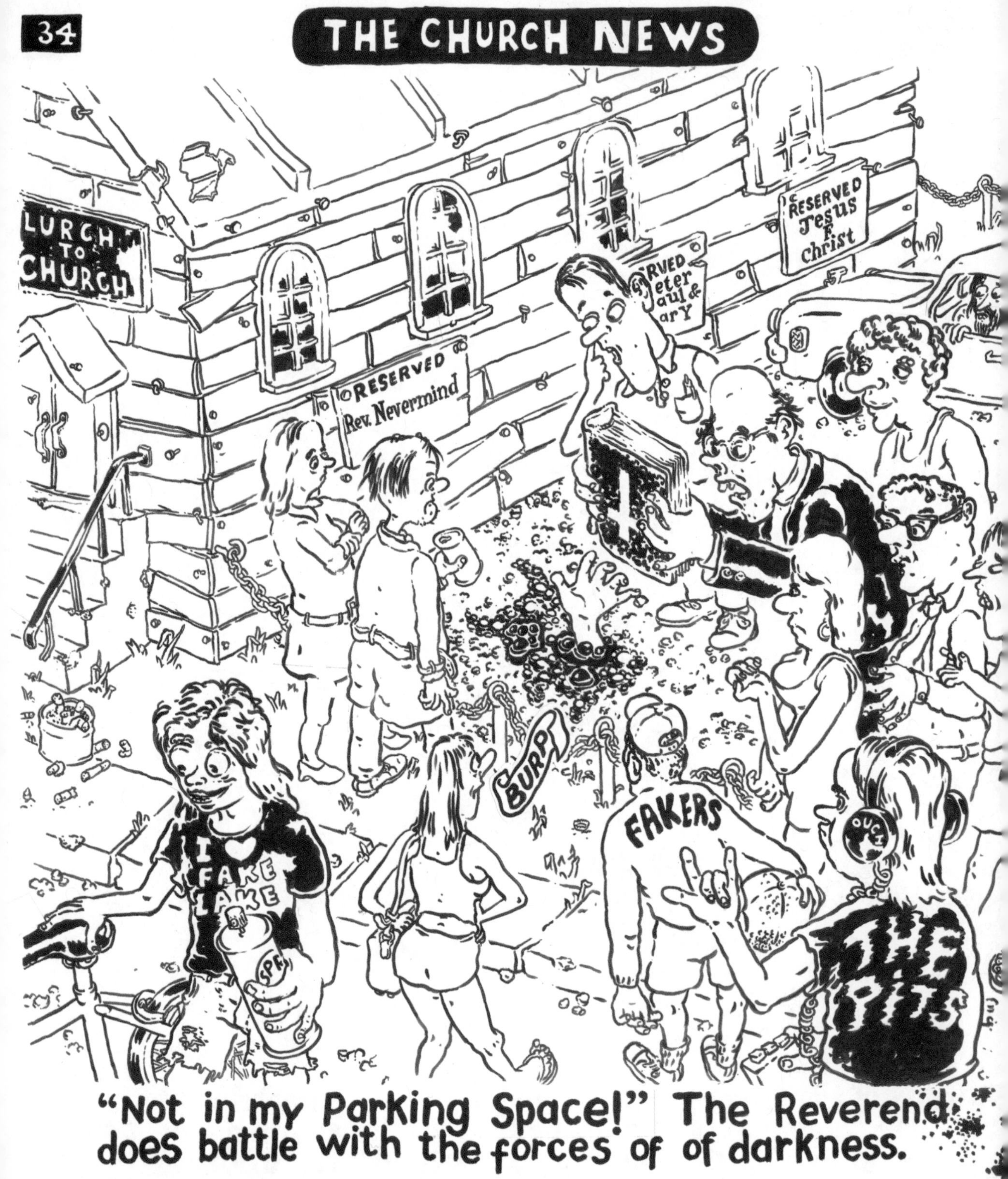
LURCH TO CHURCH
RESERVED Rev. Nevermind
RVED eter aul & ary
RESERVED Jesus F. christ
BURP
I ♥ FAKE LAKE
SPF
FAKERS
OUCH
THE PITS

"Not in my Parking Space!" The Reverend does battle with the forces of of darkness.

OPPOSING THEOLOGICAL VIEWS

"Satan has a filthy toe-hold in our Community."
-The Reverend Neverend of the Fake Lake Pentupecostal Church.

"Really, Satan's toes are quite clean. He was just in for a Pedicure last week."
-Miss Irma Emeryboard from Cut to the quick Manicure & Massage.

SATAN'S LITTLE CHAPSTICK

IT'S BUBBLING UP SATAN

A peculiar black Patch (pictured right) was discovered in the Parking lot of the church this Week. The irregular shape appears to be a Profile in silhouette of Lucifer. Two dogs, old Mrs. Holierthanthou and a bottle of communion wine that the Reverend Neverend threw in as a test all sunk without a trace. One bystander said that he heard a burp.

BURP!

UNGODLY ASPHALT

IN A HURRY FOR AN OBITUARY?

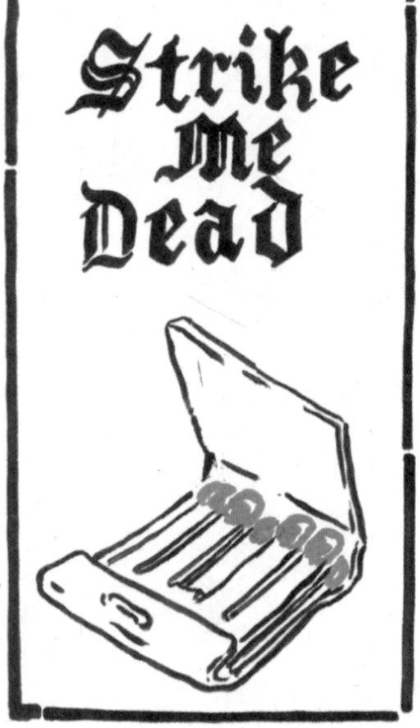
Strike
Me
Dead

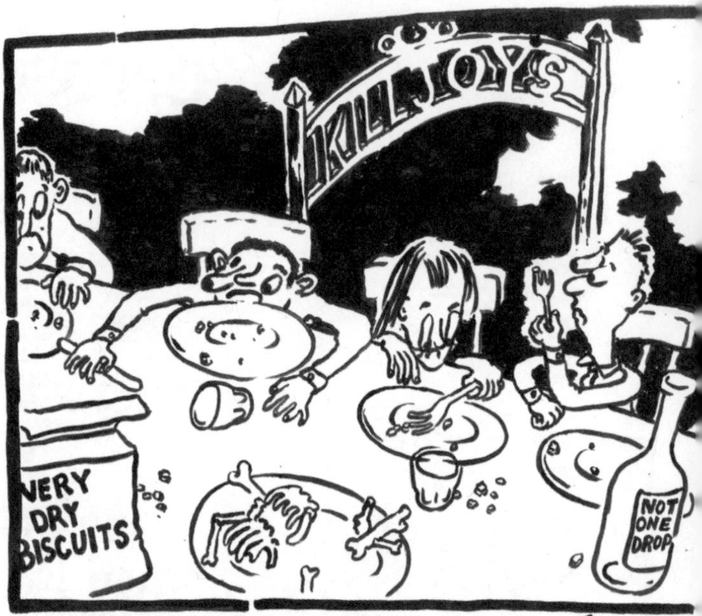
KILLJOY'S
VERY DRY BISCUITS
NOT ONE DROP

A scene from the annual KillJOY'S Orphanage "Not a Crumb" charity dinner.

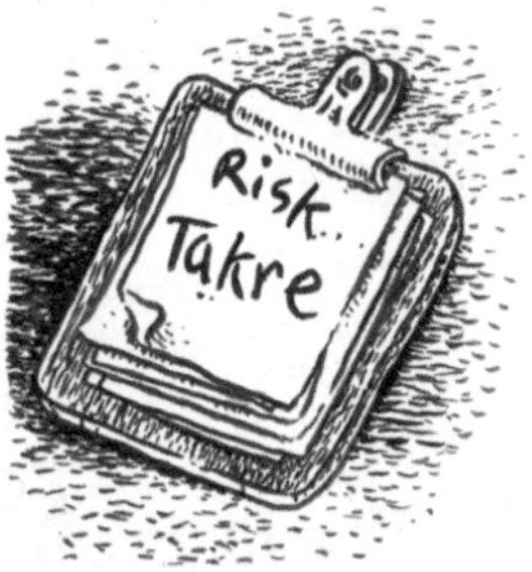
Risk Takre

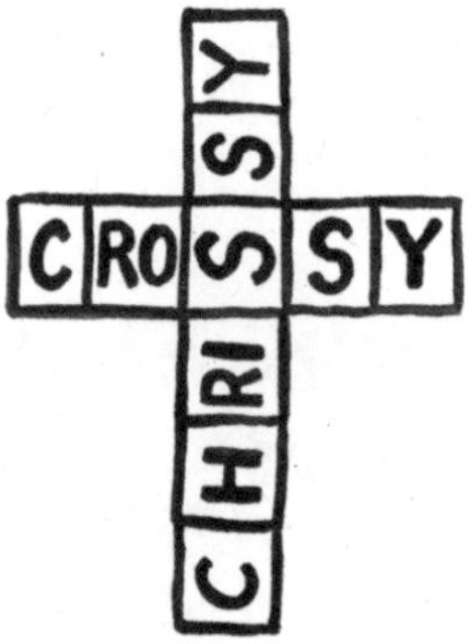
CROSSY
CHRISSY

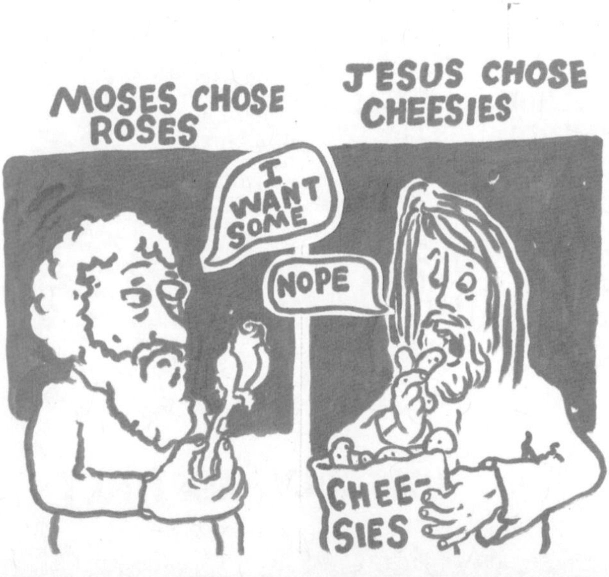
MOSES CHOSE ROSES
JESUS CHOSE CHEESIES
I WANT SOME
NOPE
CHEE-SIES

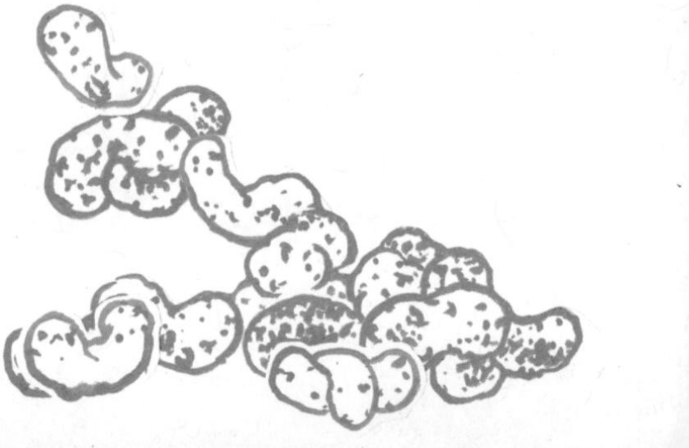

I'm Licked

IT'S REAL HOG'S BRISTLES

BRUSH WITH DEATH

Have You Had One Lately?

"I loved mine. Got rid of all the loose flaky stuff."
Mr. Dan D. Ruff

Midnight Churchyard Dig

COMPANY AT LAST

BRING A SHOVEL

IT'S A RIP OFF

SIGN UP

The Creep Twins

Mr. Epi Glottis

Dr. UPTOHISELBOWS

Miss Sarah Insalubrious

YOUR NAME

I'LL BE There

Hot Chocolate & Scones Provided by The Ladie's Benevolent Tea & Tibias Society and the Fake Lake Local Ghouls Assoc.

Dead

Miserable Dan McCombover
Thank God

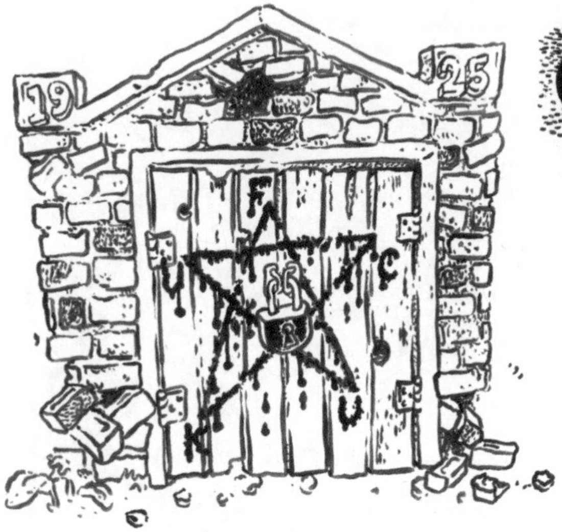
19
25

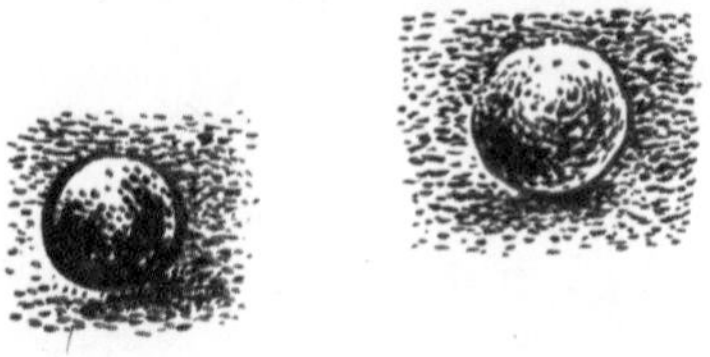

FART OF THE DEAD

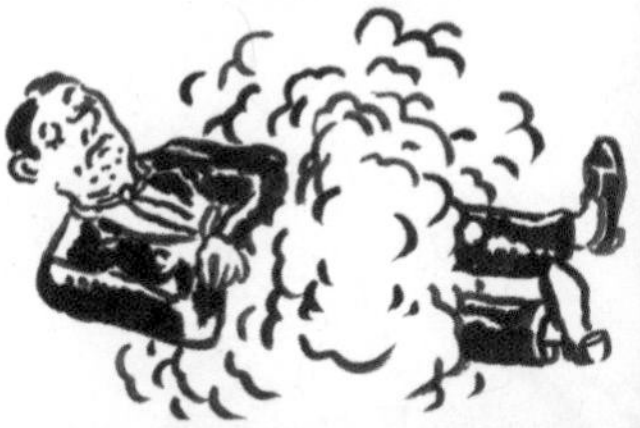

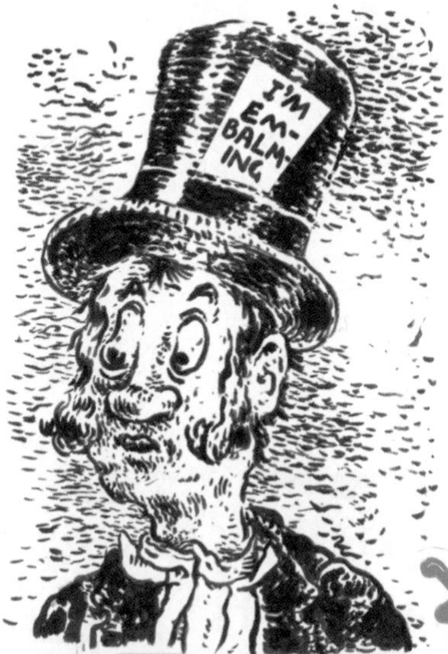
I'M EM-BALM-ING

UNDERTAKING UNDERTAKEN

OOZE GREW & GREW OOZES GREW & GREWSES

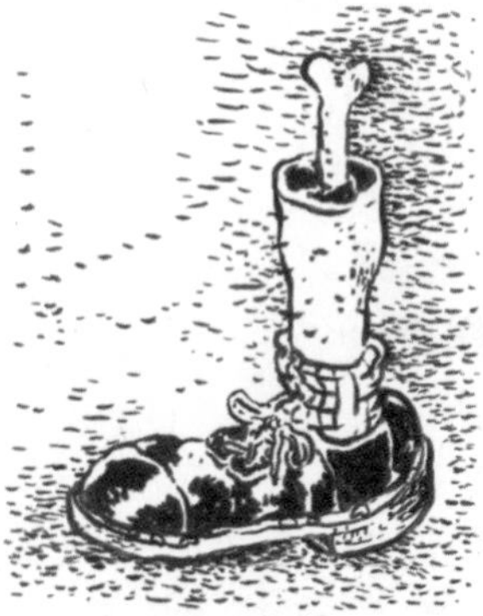

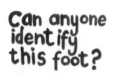

Can anyone identify this foot?

You can claim it at:
FAKE LAKE
LOST PROPERTY,
MUNICIPAL BLDG.

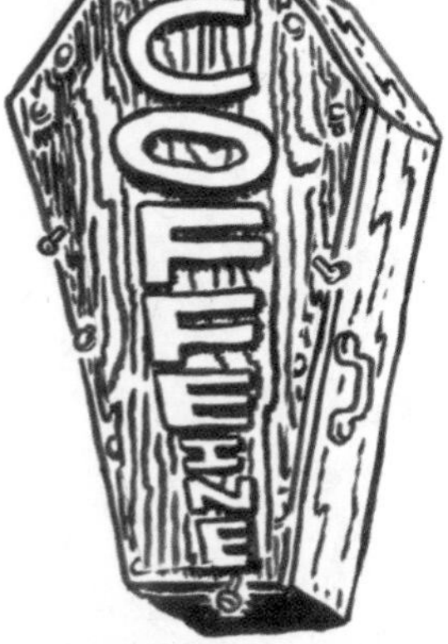

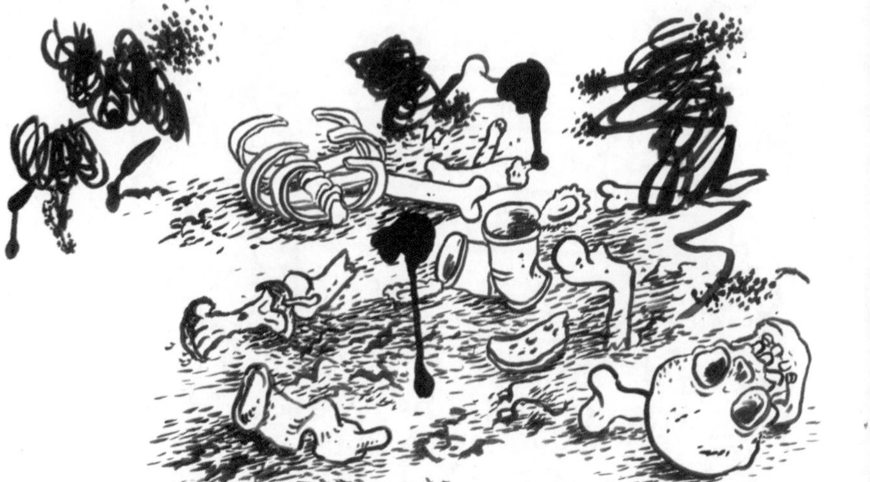

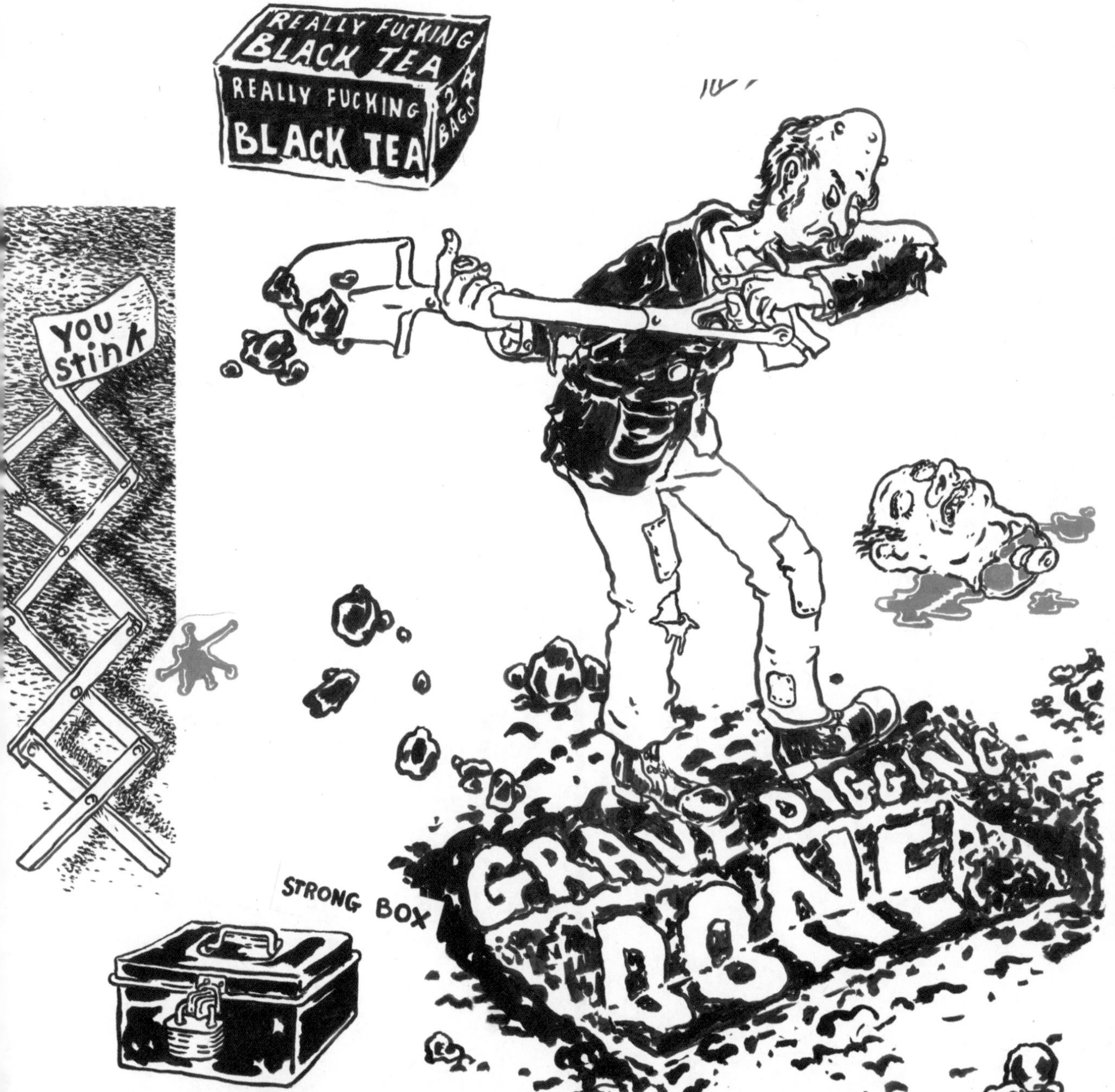
REALLY FUCKING BLACK TEA
REALLY FUCKING BLACK TEA
24 BAGS
YOU stink
STRONG BOX
GRAVE DIGGING DONE

I WILL BURY ANYFINK. COMPETERTIVE RATES. DISCRETION ASHORED. Call: Mr. Forearm, FAKE LAKE 02043 Leave a detayled message

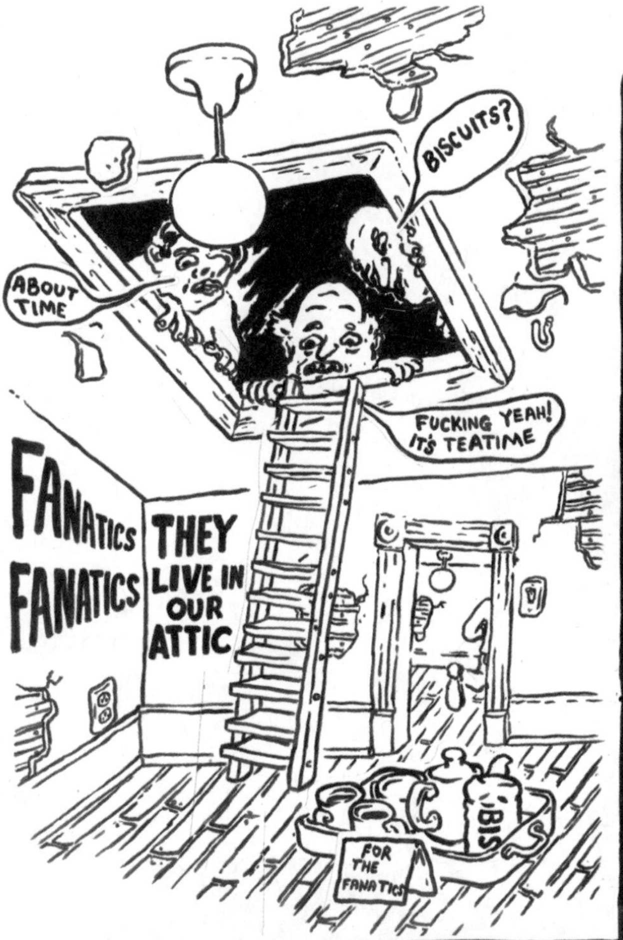
BISCUITS?
ABOUT TIME
FUCKING YEAH! IT'S TEATIME
FANATICS FANATICS
THEY LIVE IN OUR ATTIC
BIS
FOR THE FANATICS

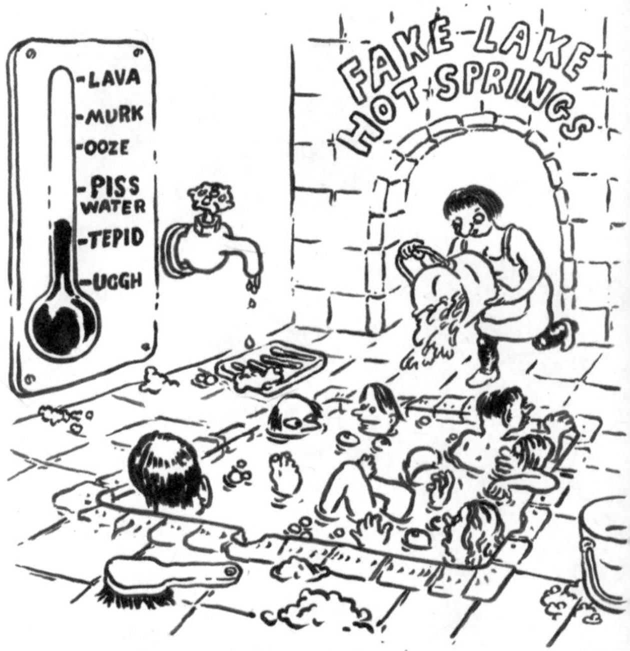
FAKE LAKE HOT SPRINGS
LAVA
MURK
OOZE
PISS WATER
TEPID
UGGH

IT'S NOT SO HOT

Patrons of the Fake Lake Hot Springs continued to soak up the waters this week despite warnings that the bacteria count had reached a new high. The amoeba bouillon was officially blamed on a bad pump but many wonder if it wasn't caused by the client's well known fondness for relieving themselves in situ.

Editor's Note: Cup-a-Soup anyone?

Fake Lake Flotsam & Jetsam

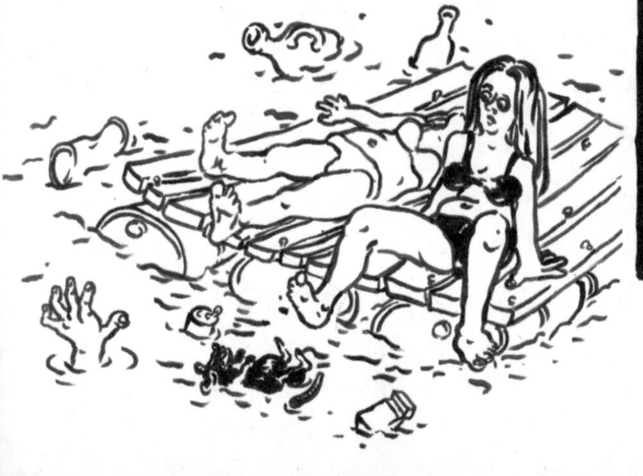

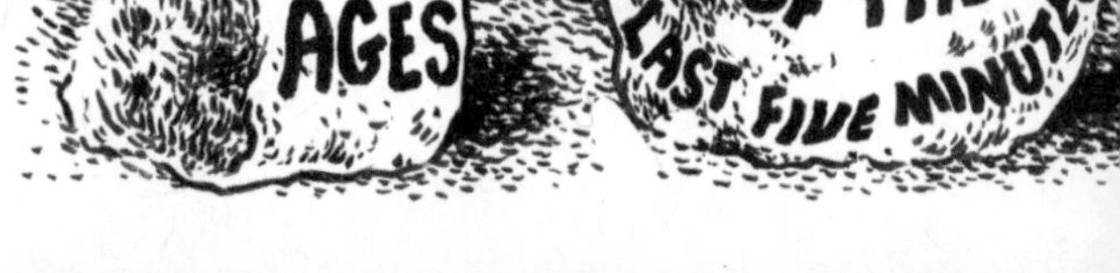
ROCK OF AGES
BOULDER OF THE LAST FIVE MINUTES

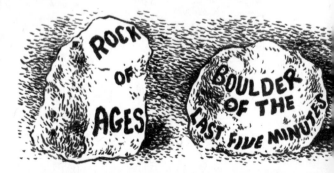

Your Society Pages

CONTINUED OVERLEAF

Dudley Sorrywad with a clutch of Doomed investments.

A Pastry Counter Encounter

NOSTRILS NO THRILLS

MR. FLESHPOT COOLING OFF

Scotsman of the Day

THE GET MORES, THE HAVE MORES

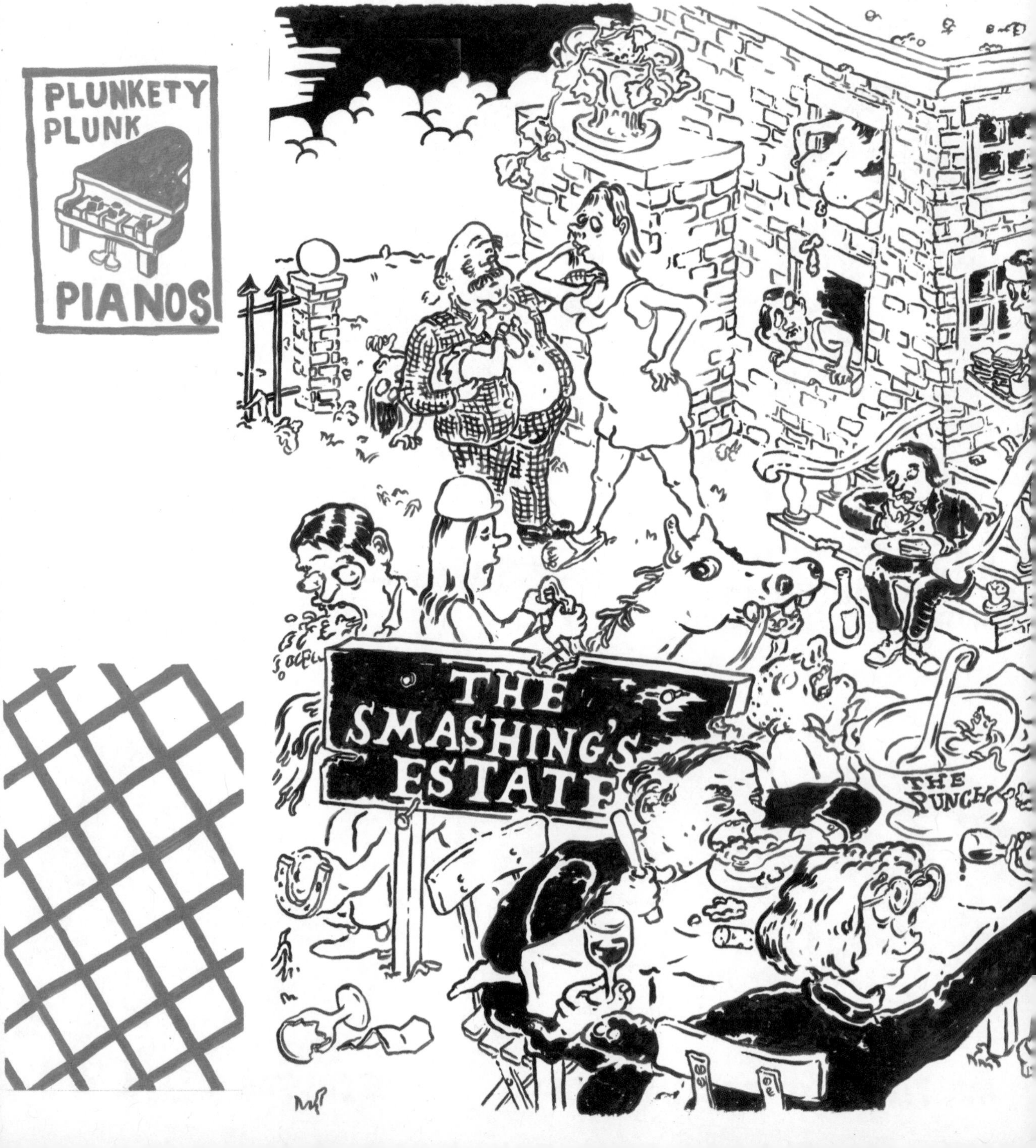
PLUNKETY PLUNK
PIANOS
THE SMASHING'S ESTATE
THE PUNCH

A Scene from Mr. & Mrs.
Smashing's garden party held last weekend. Revellers include:

- Mr. & Mrs. Smashing (top left)
- Miss Suckwell Smashing (mounted)
- Mrs. Anytakers (also mounted. On balcony with unidentified man)
- Old Mr. Tumescent Smashing (just visible on the interior of Smashing Hall)
- Miss Crownbowels (framed in the west window) and Mr. Thumprump (directly underneath)
- Mr. Portland C. Ment (seated on stairs)
- Miss Julia Cashandcarry (seated in pond)
- Miss Libby Twolips (bottom right)
- Mr. Pendulous (just visible behind Miss Twolips)
- Mr. Philip Fullofit (left of Mr. Pendulous)
- Ursula Unmanned (to the right of the Punchbowl)
- Mr. Worseforwear (punchbowl left, asleep)
- Mr. Doublegorge (awake, below)
- The Irreverend Sureswigs (bottom centre)
- Young Mr. Upchuck Smashing (far left, unwell)

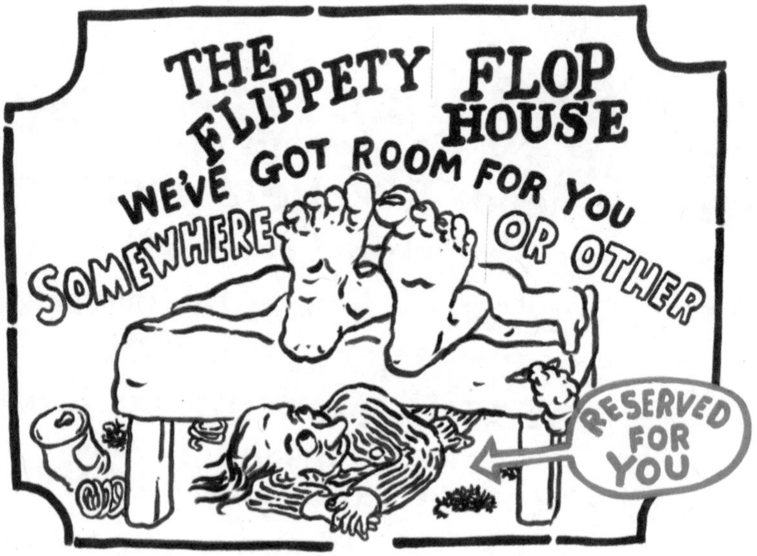
THE FLIPPETY FLOP HOUSE
WE'VE GOT ROOM FOR YOU SOMEWHERE OR OTHER
RESERVED FOR YOU

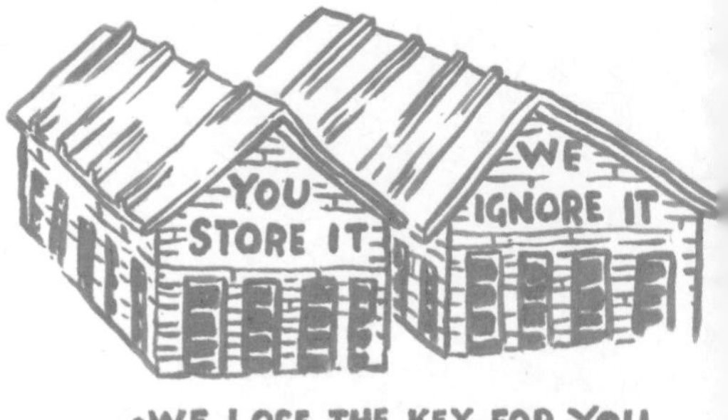
YOU STORE IT
WE IGNORE IT

- WE LOSE THE KEY FOR YOU
- WE CHANGE THE LOCKS ON YOU
- CONSIDER IT GONE
- IT'S AS GOOD AS LOST
- KISS IT GOODNIGHT
- YOU NEVER OWNED IT
- YOU'RE NEVER GETTING IT BACK

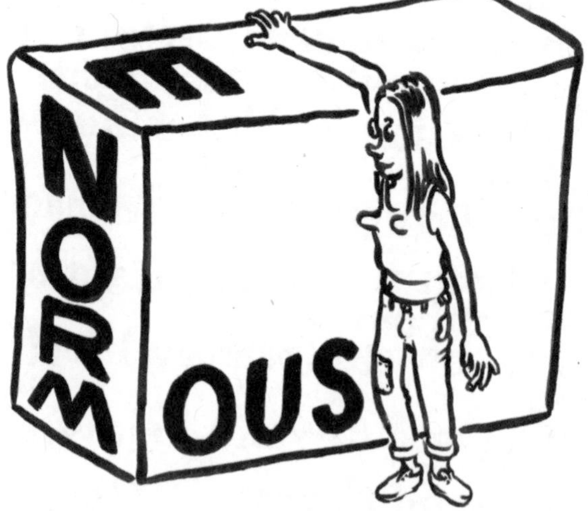
E
NORM
OUS

FAKE LAKE POST
OVERSIZED PARCELS

You didn't Know You could ship something this huge did You? And You can't, that's way too big. Get that damned thing shrunk down.

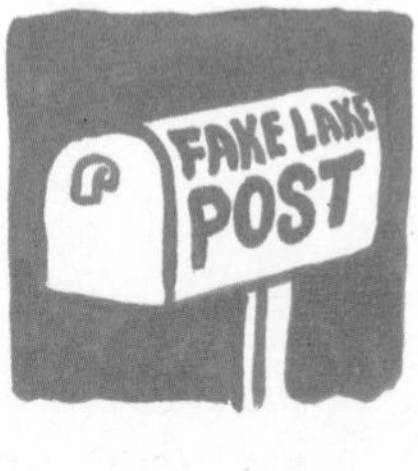
FAKE LAKE POST

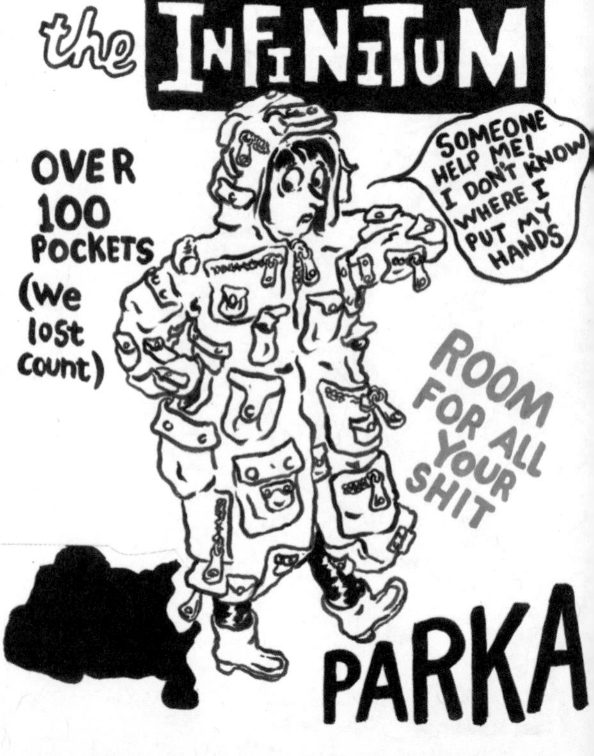
the INFINITUM
OVER 100 POCKETS (We lost count)
SOMEONE HELP ME! I DON'T KNOW WHERE I PUT MY HANDS
ROOM FOR ALL YOUR SHIT
PARKA

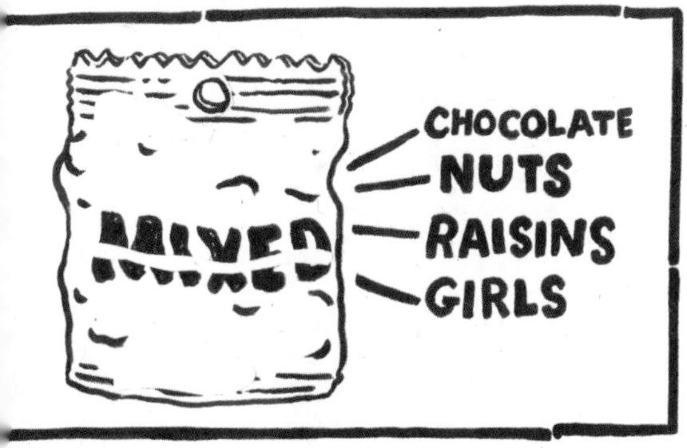
MIXED
CHOCOLATE
NUTS
RAISINS
GIRLS

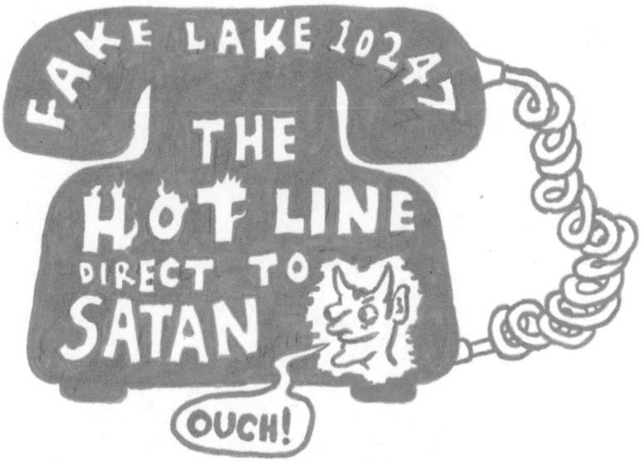
FAKE LAKE 10247
THE
HOT LINE
DIRECT TO
SATAN
OUCH!

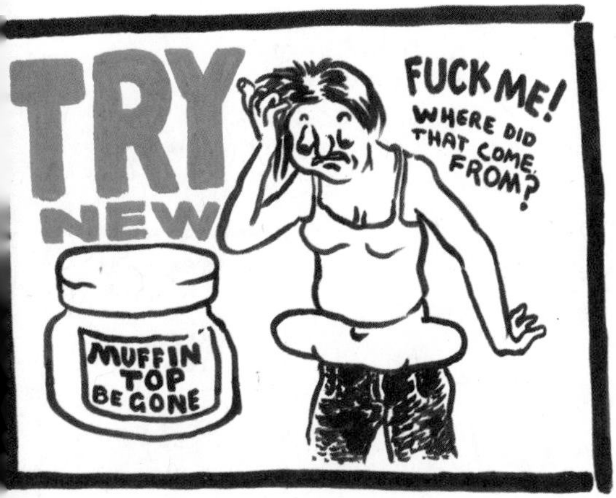
TRY
NEW
MUFFIN TOP BE GONE
FUCK ME!
WHERE DID THAT COME FROM?

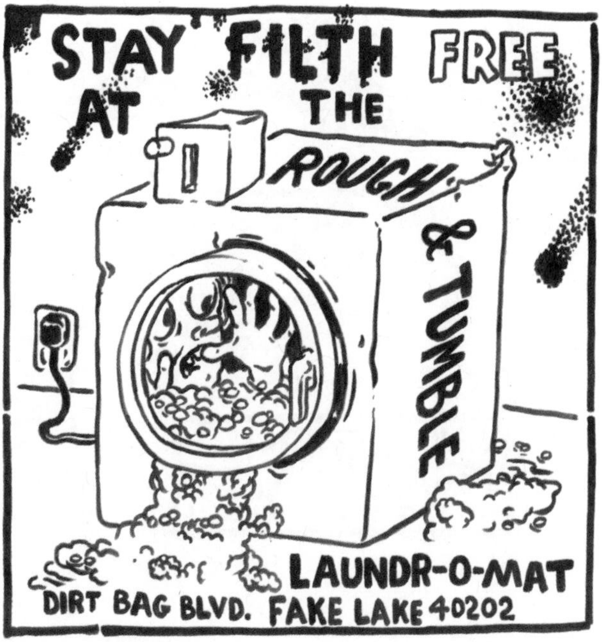
STAY FILTH FREE
AT THE
ROUGH & TUMBLE
LAUNDR-O-MAT
DIRT BAG BLVD. FAKE LAKE 40202

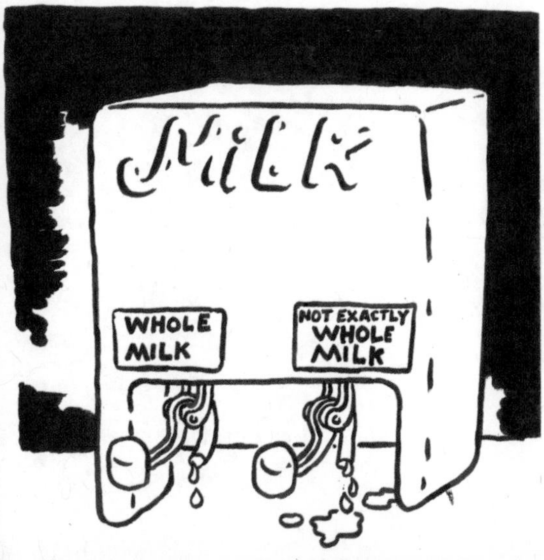
MILK
WHOLE MILK
NOT EXACTLY WHOLE MILK

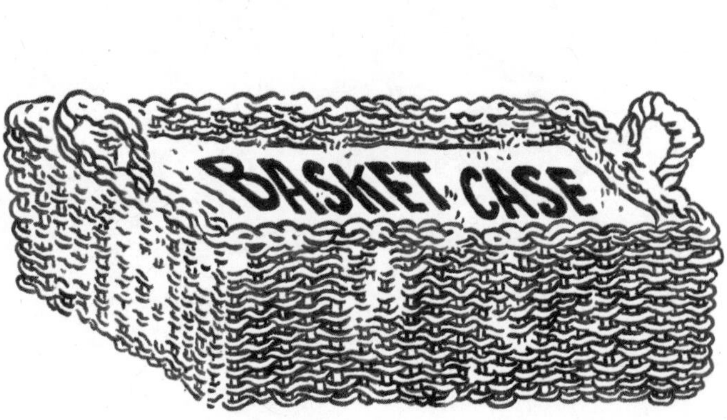
BASKET CASE

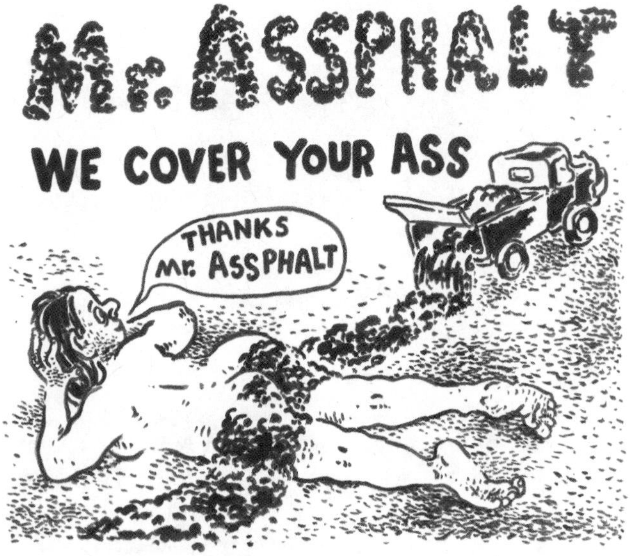
Mr. ASSPHALT
WE COVER YOUR ASS
THANKS Mr. ASSPHALT

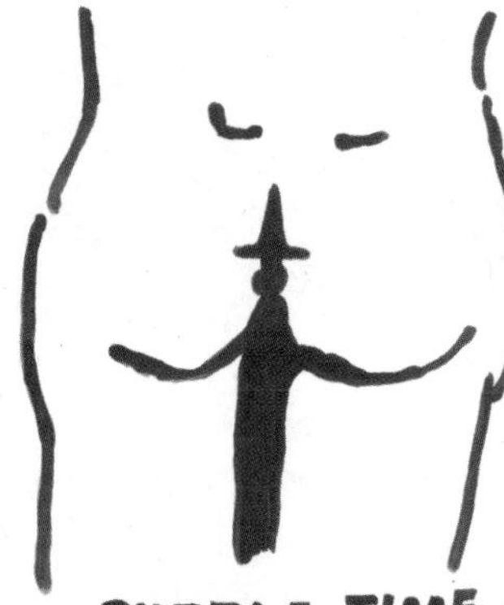

PUZZLE TIME
CAN YOU FIND:
a.) A bottom
b.) A witch
C.) My glasses. I can't see a thing without them

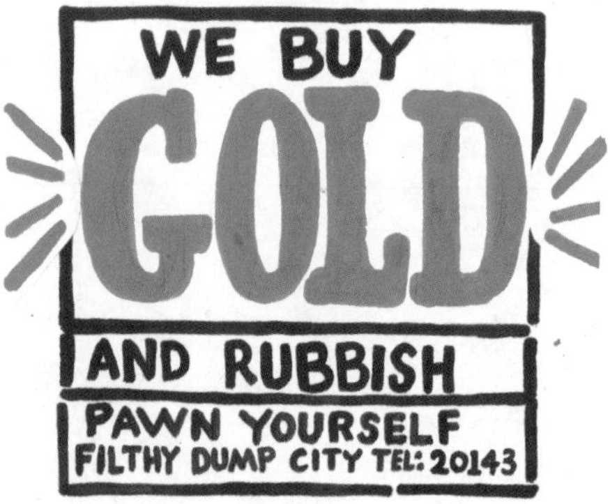
WE BUY
GOLD
AND RUBBISH
PAWN YOURSELF
FILTHY DUMP CITY TEL: 20143

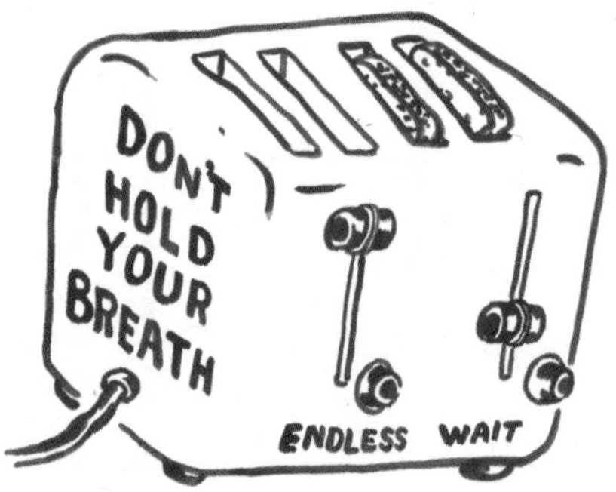
DON'T HOLD YOUR BREATH
ENDLESS
WAIT

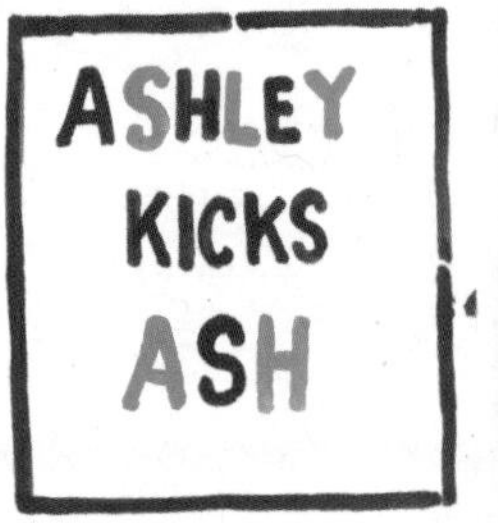
ASHLEY
KICKS
ASH

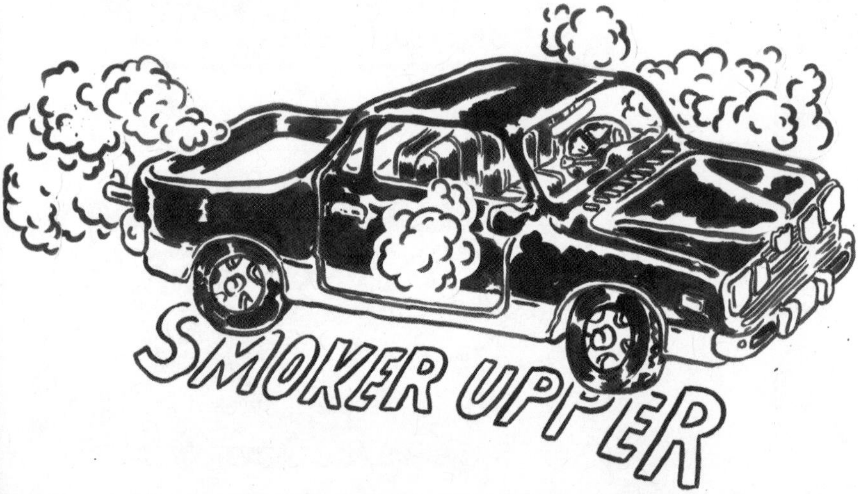
SMOKER UPPER

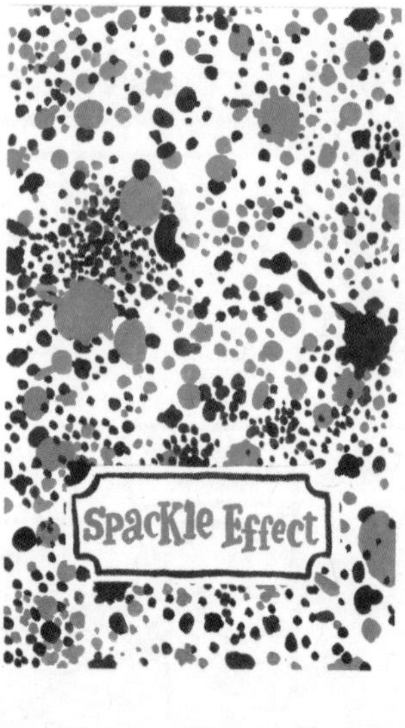
Spackle Effect

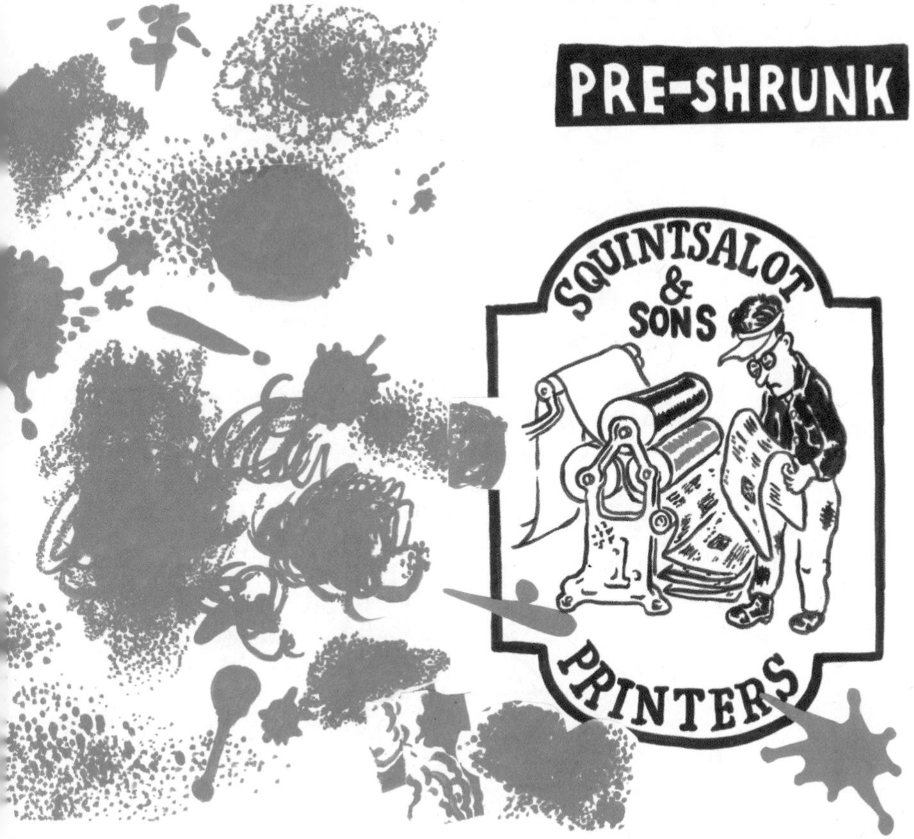
PRE-SHRUNK
SQUINTSALOT & SONS
PRINTERS

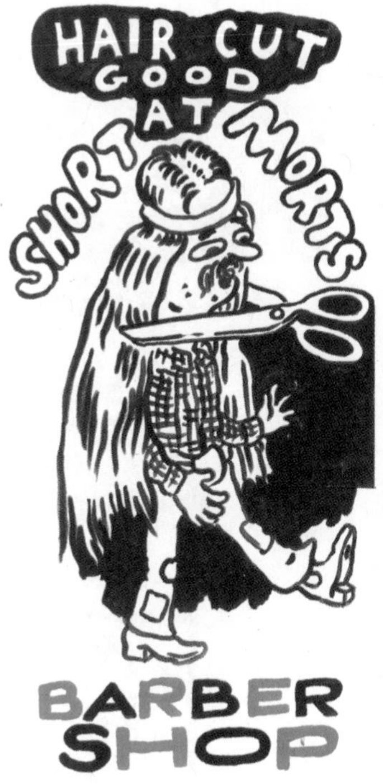
HAIR CUT GOOD AT
SHORT MORTS
BARBER SHOP

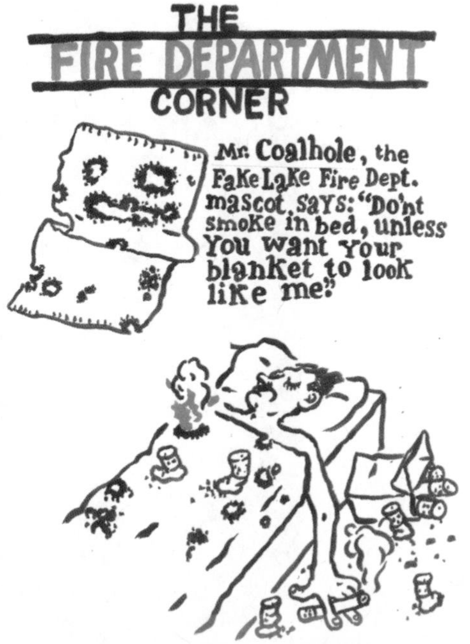
THE FIRE DEPARTMENT CORNER
Mr. Coalhole, the FakeLake Fire Dept. mascot says: "Do'nt smoke in bed, unless you want your blanket to look like me!"

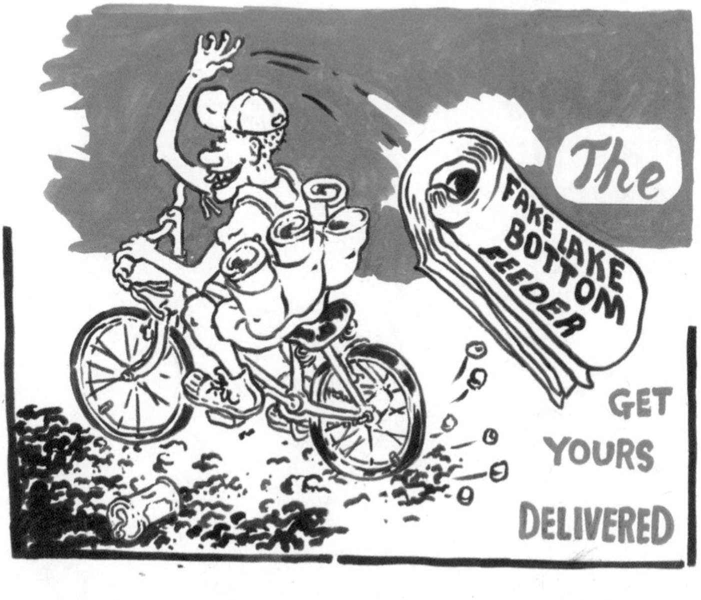
The
FAKE LAKE BOTTOM FEEDER
GET YOURS DELIVERED

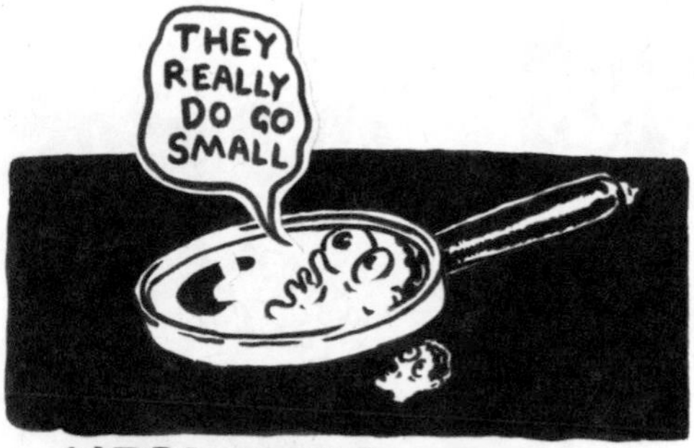
THEY REALLY DO GO SMALL

MINUTIA INC.

LOOKING FOR AN IOTA? WE HAVE LOTS. ALSO SPECKS & NUFFINKS & WIDDLY BITS. COME IN AND SEE JUST HOW SMALL WE GO.

27¼ SKINNY ALLEY (DUCK WHEN ENTERING)

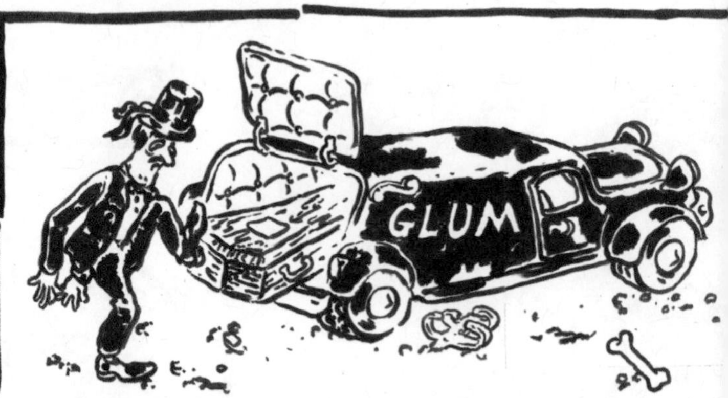
GLUM

GLUM & SONS FUNERAL SERVICES

(SUCCESSORS TO MESSRS. PICKLED & PALE)

FARTFIELD • LIQUOREDUP CITY • FILTHYDUMP CITY • FAKE LAKE

PRIVATE CHAPEL OF REST • DISCO LIGHT RENTALS

EMERGENCY CALLS

TELEPHONE HEAD OFFICE - TITTYTOWN 23995

(24 HOUR ANSAFONE & DIRTY CALLBACK SERVICE)

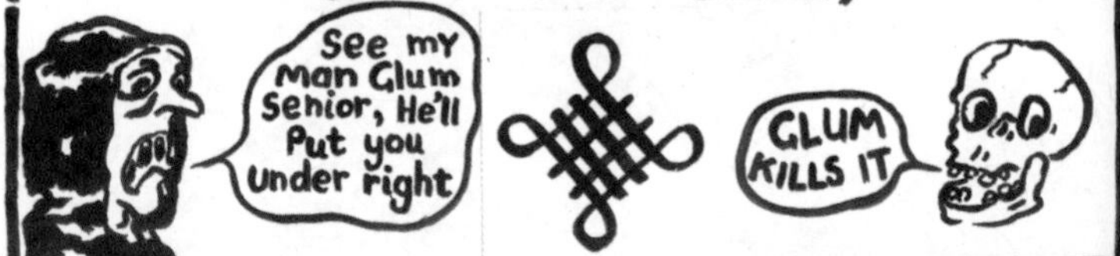
See my man Glum Senior, He'll Put you under right
GLUM KILLS IT

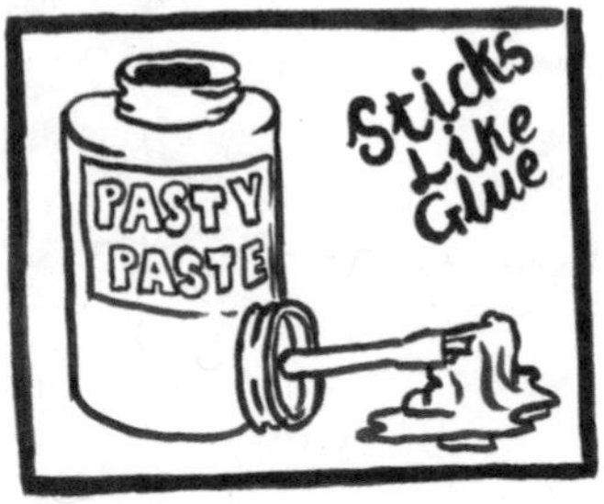
PASTY PASTE
Sticks Like Glue

FEELING FUCKING AWFUL?

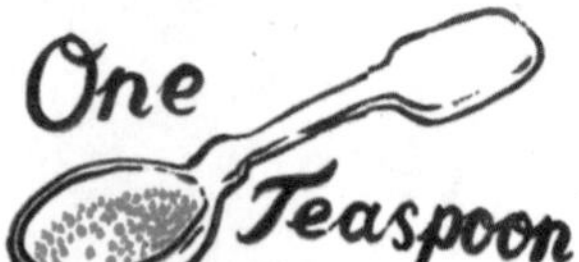
One
Teaspoon

FEELING FUCKING BETTER NOW?

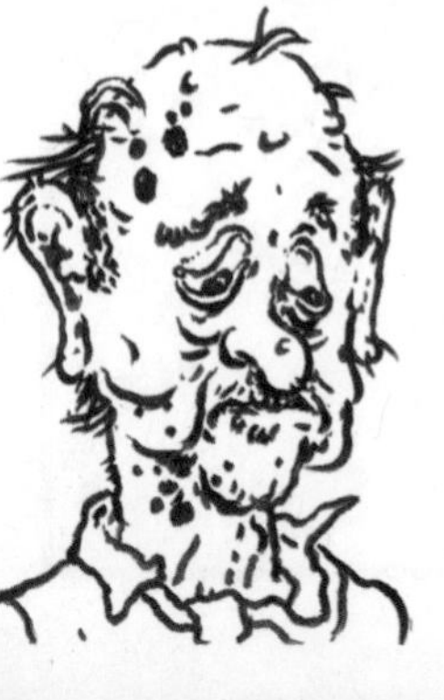

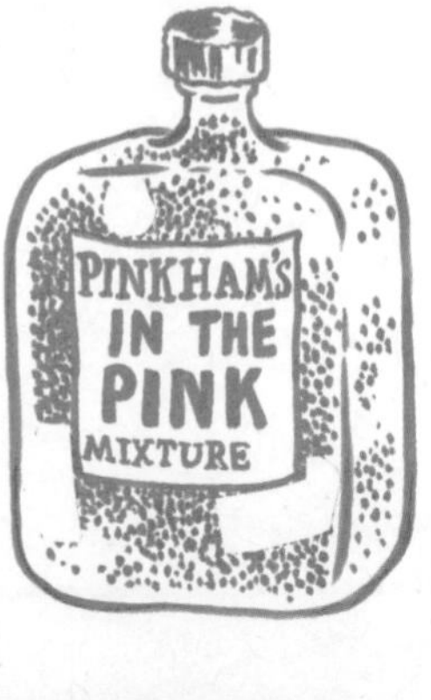
PINKHAM'S IN THE PINK MIXTURE

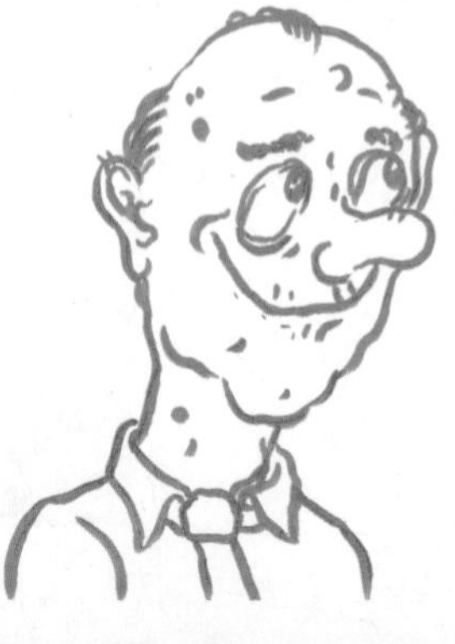

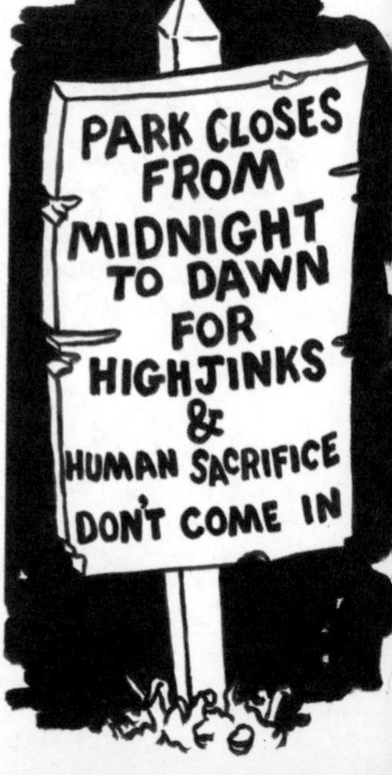
PARK CLOSES FROM MIDNIGHT TO DAWN FOR HIGHJINKS & HUMAN SACRIFICE DON'T COME IN

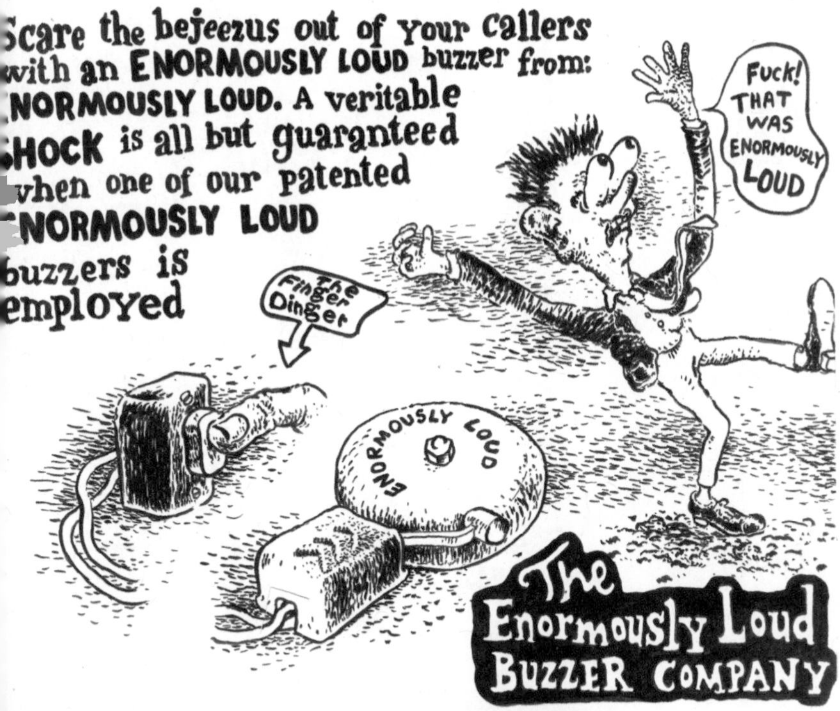
Scare the bejeezus out of your callers
with an ENORMOUSLY LOUD buzzer from:
NORMOUSLY LOUD. A veritable
HOCK is all but guaranteed
when one of our patented
NORMOUSLY LOUD
buzzers is
employed
FUCK! THAT WAS ENORMOUSLY LOUD
The Finger Dinger
ENORMOUSLY LOUD
The Enormously Loud
BUZZER COMPANY

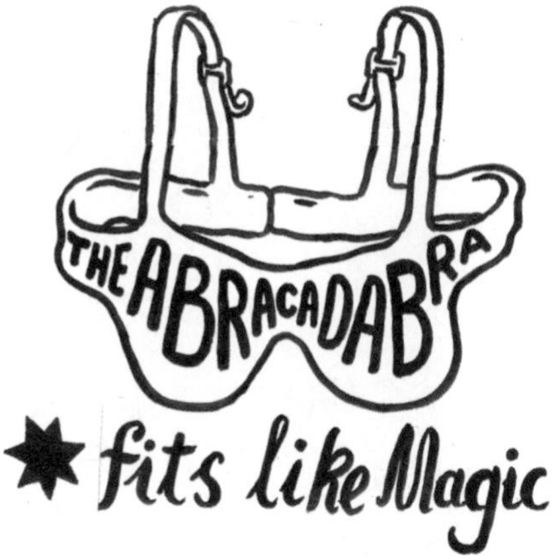
THE ABRACADABRA
fits like Magic

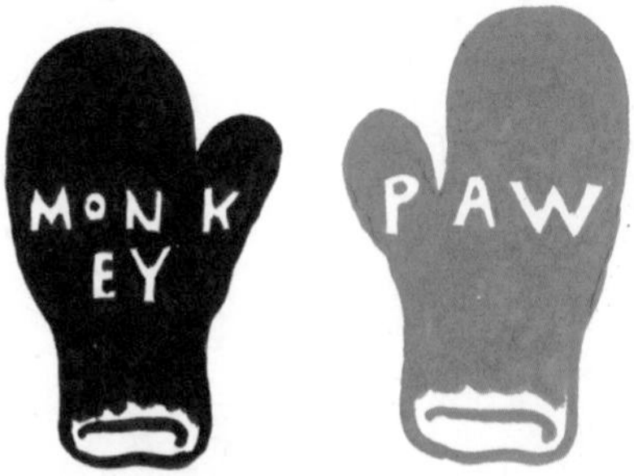
MONKEY
PAW

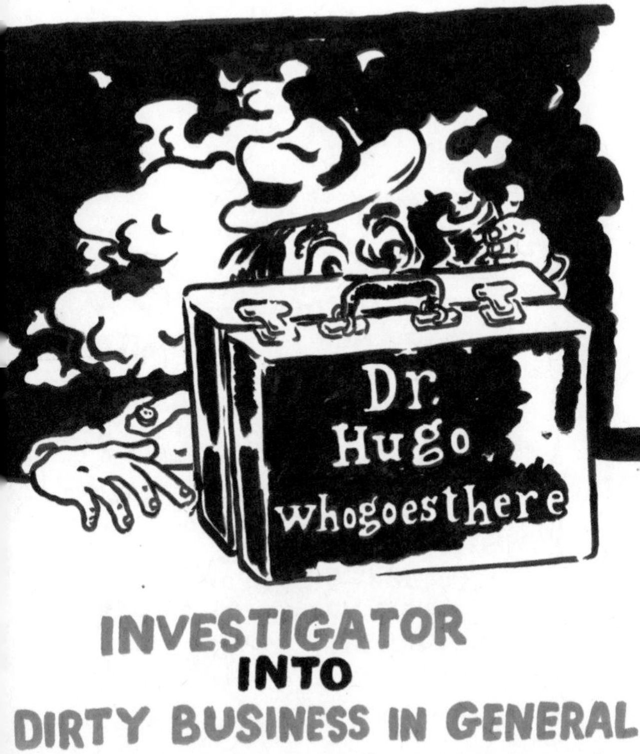
Dr. Hugo whogoesthere
INVESTIGATOR
INTO
DIRTY BUSINESS IN GENERAL

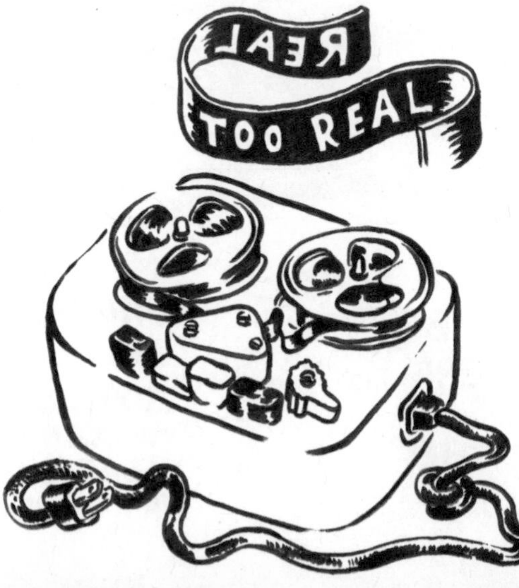
REAL
TOO REAL

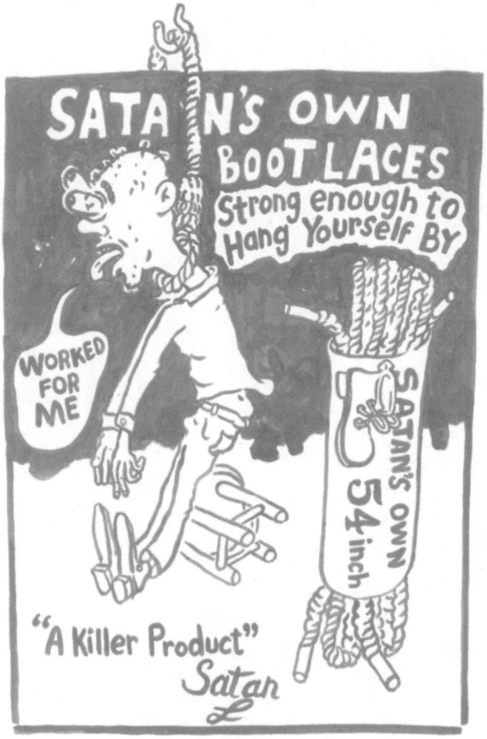
SATAN'S OWN
BOOTLACES
Strong enough to Hang Yourself By
WORKED FOR ME
SATAN'S OWN
54 inch
"A Killer Product"
Satan

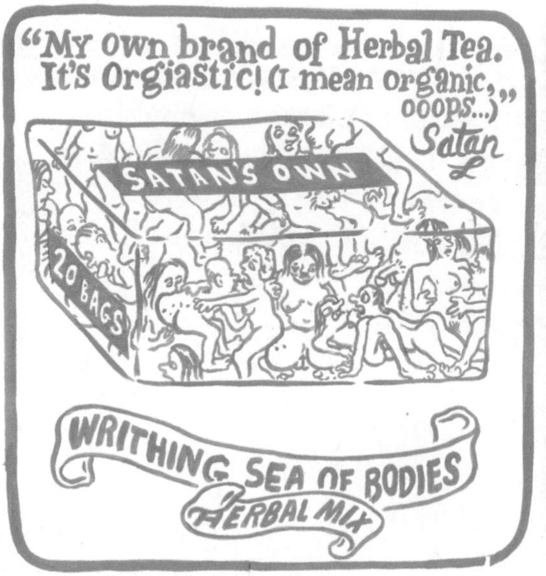
"My own brand of Herbal Tea. It's Orgiastic! (I mean organic, ooops...)"
Satan
SATAN'S OWN
20 BAGS
WRITHING SEA OF BODIES
HERBAL MIX

AVAILABLE AT THE HURRY UP AND HURRY MART IN FAKE LAKE AND AT LENTILS ON THE BRAIN HEALTH FOODS IN FILTHY DUMP CITY

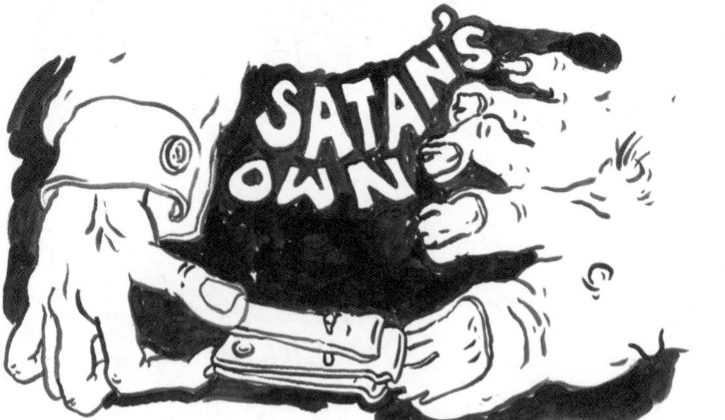
SATAN'S
OWN

SATAN'S VERY OWN-BES[T] CLIPPERS MADE TO[...] BUT THE[Y] ALMOST A[...]

THIS WAS SUPPOSED TO BE IN RED!!!
Satan

MY CLIPPERS CUT: FINGERNAILS, CLAWS, CARTILAGE, TENDONS, SINEWS, HORN, HIDE, WODDEN DOWELS, LEAD & COPPER PIPE AND SO MUCH MORE...

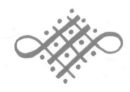

"Truly Vile"
—THE NEW YORK REVIEW OF COCKS

Miss Harriet Omelet turned her mother into a walnut and made brownies with her. You can find the Spell (and recipe) in

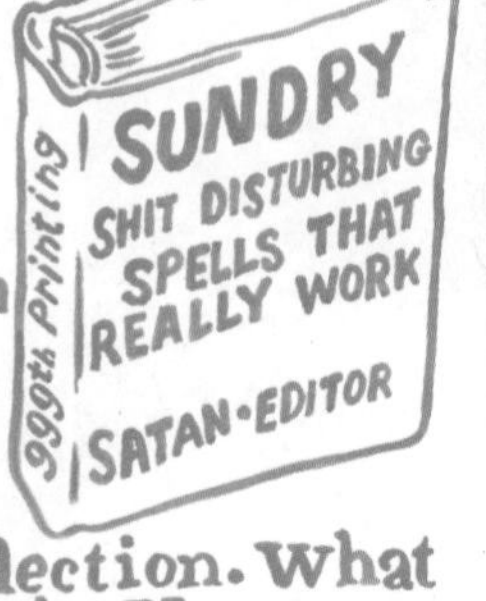
999th Printing
SUNDRY
SHIT DISTURBING
SPELLS THAT
REALLY WORK
SATAN·EDITOR

my classic collection. What Kind of havoc do You want to wreaK? Satan